MW00769524

ABSOLUTION

D.V. BERKOM

DUCT TAPE PRESS

ABSOLUTION
A Leine Basso Thriller
Copyright © 2019 by D.V. Berkom
All rights reserved.

ISBN: 978-0997970883

Published by

First print edition January 2019
Cover by Deranged Doctor Designs

Author Website: dvberkom.com

1

London, United Kingdom

Leine Basso glanced at her watch for the third time. He was supposed to be there by now. Her source was normally impeccable. She scanned the surrounding area through a pair of binoculars.

Had they been compromised?

In this old, familiar world she'd chosen to re-enter, being compromised was the default.

Part of the game.

It was not a game she enjoyed. She leaned back against the ancient, gnarled tree, drawing on logic to replace the obsessive thoughts threatening to derail her efforts.

She ran through the events that brought her to the banks of the Thames in the middle of Britain's largest city. There were no indications she or her team had been compromised. Not yet. She was letting her frustration at being unable to locate Salome get to her.

This job required patience, persistence, and reason.

Her quest to eliminate the French-born terrorist had become a singular addiction, a fixation of sorts.

Which was never good.

Remember, Leine, you're playing the long game here.

Although she'd thwarted Salome's plans less than six months earlier, Leine couldn't help feeling as though she were missing something vital, something basic, something dark. Growing and clawing its way into existence, like a misshapen thing, struggling to emerge from the sludge and sewage of the underground terrorism surge taking shape in Europe and beyond.

Careful to keep her inquiries anonymous, Leine returned to London after ranging far afield, searching for Salome under every rock she could find. Several months had passed, but she was no closer to finding her than she'd been when she started.

That was a long time in terrorist years. Salome could have changed her appearance and cobbled together enough support to launch another retinue of true believers willing to do anything to bring down a hated opponent.

"Got him." The voice of Art Kowalski, the team's overwatch, crackled through her earpiece. "He's on the bridge." A semi-retired security specialist and former CIA operative, Art had been her go-to in Greece the year before.

Leine scanned Tower Bridge for the man known only as the Bomb Maker. He was to meet with Daniel, one of Art's most trusted operatives. Wired for sound, Daniel had agreed to act as the buyer. At the moment, the sensitive recording device camouflaged as a button on his light blue oxford shirt was picking up the tourist chatter streaming past him on the bridge.

Approaching from the south, Daniel made his way through the throngs of tourists to where the Bomb Maker waited next to the railing midway across the bridge. The unusually hot summer had segued into a cool, damp fall, and both men were dressed in slacks and overcoats. The cadaverous Bomb Maker wore a neck scarf, a wool fisherman's cap, and a pair of leather gloves, while Daniel, shorter and on the stocky side, wore a knit watchman's cap but no gloves or scarf.

"Is the Thames always so muddy?" Daniel asked, delivering the first line in the agreed-upon code to establish bona fides.

"Sometimes it's as dark as chocolate," answered the Bomb Maker.

The Bomb Maker lifted his chin in acknowledgement and stepped closer to Daniel. "I need to verify the order."

Daniel had requested the man's specialty—an easily transported bomb capable of delivering structural failure to any one of the bridges jutting across the Thames. Strangely enough, the Bomb Maker had resisted Daniel's initial request for a bespoke explosive to take out the bridge they were currently standing on. When pressed for a reason, the Bomb Maker simply said if he were ever connected to the destruction of such a historic site in London it wouldn't be good for business.

"I can have it ready for you by Tuesday," the bomber said.

"Tuesday is good. How do you want the money?"

The man paused for a moment before answering. "Small denomination, unmarked euros. Put the money in a duffel bag and hide it in the bushes behind the northernmost bench in Trinity Park on Tower Hill."

"Half now, half when you deliver, right?" Daniel asked.

"All of it. By tomorrow morning."

Leine scanned the bridge through her binoculars, searching for anyone who appeared to be watching the Bomb Maker's back. Several feet from the two men stood a guy with dark hair and a black peacoat who didn't look like a tourist. He'd appeared around the time of the meet and hadn't moved from his position.

"I'll pay half. Nothing more until delivery."

"Then our business is finished." The Bomb Maker started to leave.

"Wait." Daniel's voice was just the right amount of anxious.

The other man stopped and turned.

"I'll get you the money. By tomorrow."

The Bomb Maker nodded, once. "Leave it at the drop by ten o'clock tomorrow morning."

"Where will we meet when it's ready?"

"I'll contact you."

"How?"

The Bomb Maker narrowed his eyes. "You ask too many questions."

Back off, Daniel. He's getting squirrelly. Leine tightened her grip on the binoculars.

Daniel shrugged, nodded. "I get it. You'll find me."

"Yes." The Bomb Maker appeared to think for a moment. "Who did you say you worked for?"

"I didn't." Daniel's tone was neutral, neither wary nor friendly.

Jamie, one of Art's guys, walked past them, but Daniel kept his focus on the Bomb Maker. In contrast, the Bomb Maker glanced after the man and lifted his chin. The guy in the black peacoat waited for Art's operative to walk past before he turned to follow.

"One of our guys just picked up a tail," Leine muttered into her mic.

"Copy that. Jamie, watch your back," Art warned.

Jamie keyed his mic twice.

Leine refocused on Daniel and the other man.

"Who do you work for?" the Bomb Maker asked again.

"That's none of your concern," Daniel replied. This time his tone had changed to one of annoyance.

"But it is." The Bomb Maker took another step closer to

Daniel and added, "It is my business to understand who I am dealing with."

"Stand by," Art said, his voice clear in Leine's earpiece. "This could go sideways."

"There's a large group coming up behind Daniel," Leine warned. Several smiling, chatting Japanese tourists were walking *en masse* toward the two men and were about to overtake them.

Daniel leaned in close to the other man. "My employer prefers to remain anonymous," he said in a low voice.

The Bomb Maker held his hands up as if in surrender and took a step back. At the same moment the group of Japanese tourists streamed past. In their midst was a man of medium height in a dark green jacket who didn't look Japanese.

"Watch the man behind you," Leine warned. At that moment, the man bumped hard into Daniel.

"What the—?" Daniel managed. The man in the green jacket threw something over the railing into the river before shoving his hands into his pockets and dissolving into the crowd. The Bomb Maker turned and quickly strode away in the opposite direction.

"Shit," Daniel wheezed.

"What? What's going on? Daniel, talk to me." Heart thudding, Leine sprinted toward the bridge. *What the hell just happened?*

There was no reply.

2

"**D**anny, what happened? Are you all right? Report."
The intensity of Art's concern spurred Leine on.

She ran past the milling tourists, pushing aside those who got in her way while she kept her focus on Daniel, who was now doubled over and leaning against the bridge railing. She reached him as he dropped to one knee, gripping his side. Another of Art's guys joined them, breathing hard from the sprint.

"Knife," Daniel managed as he reached for the railing to help him stand.

Art's guy wrapped Daniel's arm around his neck and hoisted him to his feet. The knife had entered the left side of his torso. A dark stain bloomed on the light blue oxford as pedestrians streamed past. Other than some curious looks, no one paid attention to the trio near the railing.

"He needs a medic. Now," Leine said into her mic. "Here—" She removed her wool scarf and pressed it to the injury. "Hold it against the wound."

Daniel nodded. "The fucker stabbed me in broad daylight," he wheezed. He peeled the scarf away to look—it was covered in blood. He put it back. "Looks like I've been blown," he said in a half-hearted attempt at humor.

"Yeah." Leine glanced in the direction the Bomb Maker had gone, but he was nowhere to be seen. "Art—do you have eyes on him?"

"Affirmative," Art replied. "He's headed north toward Tower Hill." He was referring to the infamous patch of ground where those unlucky enough to be deemed traitors to the crown had been put to death centuries before.

"What about the guy who knifed him?"

"I've got Thomas shadowing him."

"I'm going after the bomber."

"Zarko'll cover your six. Be careful."

"Copy that." Leine took off at a sprint in pursuit of the Bomb Maker. "What about the guy in the black coat?"

"Negative," Jamie said over the comms. "He disappeared before I could get a bead on him."

She sped past the crowd of tourists queuing up for the Tower of London. The year-round crowds made the surrounding area ideal for a meet. Especially for the terrorist responsible for the explosives that destroyed much of the Pont de l'Alma in Paris six months before. More escape routes were available by blending into a crowd than by meeting someone on a lonely stretch of road.

A few minutes later, Leine caught sight of her quarry. He was moving swiftly through Trinity Park, headed for the financial district. Zarko had caught up and was paralleling her. A tall, heavily tattooed Greek dressed in black with long dark hair, Zarko sported several piercings and a razor-sharp goatee, and was one of the best operatives around. Surprisingly, he blended into crowds well.

The Bomb Maker was key to finding Salome, the woman responsible for the Paris terrorist attack. Although she'd used other names, Leine always thought of her as Salome—the original moniker the terrorist had used when she helped a Russian general carry out a sarin gas attack in a Las Vegas casino the year before.

The Bomb Maker turned left past a public ale house and then down a narrow cobblestone street. Leine stayed several meters behind him. Zarko was nowhere in sight, but she knew he was close by.

They continued this way for a few more blocks before the Bomb Maker disappeared into a nondescript brick building set on a sparsely traveled side street. Leine pulled out her phone and searched for the address. It was listed as an apartment building with several units available for short-term rental. She walked by, noting the call box next to the double glass doors.

"He just went into an apartment building on Portsoken Street," she said into her mic. "I'll check it out." She circled the block searching for another exit. There was only one other door that opened onto a sidewalk leading to the adjacent parking lot and the building's rubbish containers. She studied the surrounding area and chose a position just down the walkway near a gym. The remaining foliage of the evenly spaced trees planted along the sidewalk gave her a modicum of cover while still allowing her a good visual of the door.

"I've got you and the building covered." Zarko's deep baritone came through the mic. "Looks clean."

"Copy that." Glad to know she hadn't been tailed and that there was no one to be concerned about nearby, Leine made herself comfortable.

In service to her obsession to kill Salome, Leine had publicly cut ties with everyone she loved, including her daughter, April; Lou Stokes, her handler at SHEN, an anti-trafficking agency; and Santiago Jensen, detective for LAPD Robbery Homicide Division and the love of her life.

The last one had been the most difficult.

She'd stopped Salome from achieving her ends twice. The first time, Leine had learned of the Russian general's grandiose campaign to lure the US into war with Russia, cutting short Salome's ambitions to be the most notorious terrorist in the world. In the second instance, she'd thwarted the terrorist's plans to destroy European landmarks in a heinous attempt at building her reputation on the world stage. Salome had learned Leine's identity and role in the Russian incident through an old contact who had suggested taking out a contract on her. It was then that Leine realized she had to break ties with her most important relationships, knowing that Salome would stop at nothing to get to Leine, including using those she loved.

Her daughter April knew Leine would be back—growing up with an assassin for a mother gave her a unique set of coping skills that would get her through. And Lou Stokes was used to her disappearing for weeks or months at a time. Although she'd publicly expressed her plans to sever all connections with the anti-trafficking agency, he'd known it was for public consumption and that she'd be in touch, however covertly.

But she had decided to make the break real with Santa. In Leine's opinion, he was the most vulnerable of her contacts. She couldn't be certain he'd act like he'd just been through a breakup if she didn't actually do it—he was too loyal, too by the numbers. If he knew there was still a chance for them to be together, he'd never take the natural step of being with someone else. Leine's heart was in shreds at ending their relationship, but it was the only way. Salome would be able to spot that kind of deception with ease.

Leine just hoped the public break would be enough.

Twenty-three minutes later, the Bomb Maker reappeared behind the glass front doors. He hesitated as he peered at the parking lot before he emerged from the building carrying a duffel bag. He turned left at the door and headed for the street, his gaze constantly moving, never settling on anything or anyone for long, as he walked through the security gate onto the sidewalk.

He hadn't seen her.

Letting him get a head start, she loosened her ponytail, allowing her dark auburn hair to cascade over her shoulders. She took off her jacket and reversed it, changing the fabric from black to brown, slipped a beige scarf from her bag and covered her head, then donned a pair of large sunglasses to throw him off in case he'd caught a glimpse of her on the bridge. Then she resumed tracking him.

He stopped at a light near a busy street, and Leine slowed her pace, staying near the back of the crowd waiting to cross. The light changed, and the mass of people moved into the intersection. Leine went with the flow, keeping the Bomb Maker in sight. Just then, a horn blared and a late-model Opel careened through the intersection. Screams erupted and pedestrians scattered, creating mass confusion. Leine had to move quickly to avoid being hit by the speeding car, and temporarily lost sight of her quarry. Out of the corner of her eye she spotted Zarko jogging across the street, close on the Bomb Maker's tail.

Seconds later the Opel sped off, and Leine raced to the other side of the intersection. She stopped and scanned the street. Zarko was halfway down the block, headed her way and shaking his head.

"Someone was waiting for him in a black sedan."

The Bomb Maker was gone.

3

A hotel in Paris—six months earlier

"What do you mean, you need space?" The hurt in Santiago Jensen's eyes was enough to rip Leine's heart in half. She was surprised there was no blood seeping from her shirt.

"I have to go it alone. The last job took too much."

"That's why you need me now." Santa moved toward her, concern etching his face. Leine shook her head and stepped back.

"No. Don't make this harder than it already is." She fought the impulse to wrap him in her arms and never let go, letting the world spin without them.

But that would be foolish, and Santa would die.

"Then talk to me."

Leine sighed. She owed him something for all the happiness they'd shared. "I've had a lot of time to think lately, and I keep coming to the same conclusion. I'm not good for you."

Santa crossed his arms and leaned against the dresser. "And why is that?"

"You know what I've done. What I do."

"Yeah, so?"

"You're a cop. Law and order. Rules and regs. Everything in its place."

"Your point?"

"I'm not." Leine closed her eyes, trying to think of the right way to say what she needed to say. "If I'm restricted by rules, I can't do my job."

Santa scoffed. "You've done just fine so far."

"No, Santa. I haven't. I've gone too far to come back."

His expression softened and he took another step toward her. She shook her head and he stopped.

"I forgive you, whatever you've done," he said. "You work for an agency that rescues children from sex traffickers. I doubt you're the only one who's gone too far."

He wasn't going to make this easy, was he? With a sigh, Leine went over to her laptop and pressed several keys. The screen filled with photographs. She stood back and gestured for him to look.

He walked over to see what she wanted to show him. His eyes narrowed and he frowned.

"What's this?" He nodded toward the grisly collage.

"My kill wall."

"Your—" He glanced back at the screen. His expression changed from concern to shock as understanding lit his face. He stared at the photographs. "So these are trophies?"

"In a sense, yes." Leine pointed to one showing a man lying on a floor, eyes staring unseeing above him, a jagged wound across his throat. Blood soaked his torso. "That's the man I killed when I found Chessa." An American teenager, Chessa had been lured to an Izz Al-Din training camp to become a terrorist bride. Leine had rescued her, killing her handler in the process.

"But you had to kill him to rescue her."

Leine pointed to another that showed three men laid shoulder to shoulder, all dead, all lined up together for a group photo. "Those three were only peripherally responsible for the kidnapping and sale of twin sisters to a human trafficking ring based out of Las Vegas."

"But you had a good reason." Santa was reaching, she could tell.

So could he.

She shook her head. "Not really. I decided to kill them because they were part of the organization. They were no threat to me or the twins."

"Still, they were part of the problem."

"You don't see it, do you? What I am, what I've done, is affecting your own belief in the law, your respect for it, how you serve it. You're willing to excuse me crossing lines."

"Because I love you and trust you're doing what needs to be done."

She pointed to a particularly gruesome photograph. This one was hard even for her to look at. It was of a middle-aged couple, their faces bashed to unrecognizable pulp. A bent fireplace poker lay next to the man in whose hand rested a Glock 32. She didn't give him the chance to fire. She'd never experienced such fury before or since. She hoped she never would again.

Santa winced. "What did they do?"

"They ran a porn site. Live streamed infants being sexually abused for subscribers. They had a professional studio in their barn."

Being a veteran cop, he'd likely seen or heard of the practice. The look on his face told her his inner compass was swinging wildly, searching for firmer ground. He would have arrested them and brought them to trial.

She beat their heads in.

She continued. "It was quite the going concern. They had a

massive investment portfolio." Leine had made sure the feds knew about the account. Anonymously, of course. Most of the subscribers had been slapped with one charge or another.

"I get it, Leine. You've done some things you're not proud of. So have I." His voice had less conviction than before. "But it's in service to good."

"But what you've done is not the same. There's a limit to how far you'll go before you cross a line."

Santa bowed his head, deep in thought. He was close—teetering on the edge. It amazed her that he was still trying to accept what she'd done. What she did. She just had to tip him over. Shoving deep the pain of losing him, she compartmentalized the shreds of her heart so she could finish the job.

"I don't feel anything when I kill." There. She'd laid her cards on the table. She'd become that which she'd always fought. A killing machine with no emotion, no ability for empathy.

Santa stared at her a long time. "Have you thought about talking to someone? I know a good psychoanalyst—"

Leine slammed the laptop cover down. "You don't get it, do you? I'm damaged goods. I'll never be what you need."

"You're everything I need." The determination in his voice was still there. "Don't I get a say in this relationship?"

Tears pricked Leine's eyelids. Her heart was shredded. What more could she say? If she didn't leave soon she'd surrender and allow him to grant her absolution for her sins. No, she had to push him away. Had to leave.

Or else he'd die.

"Well, I need more than you." She almost choked on the words, but they did what the kill wall hadn't. The stricken expression on his face was more than she could bear. She busied herself shutting down the laptop. Tucking it under her arm, she turned to say goodbye. His stunned look told her he'd finally accepted she was leaving.

"You're really going to throw everything away? Didn't our time together mean anything to you?" His voice was low, but anger sparked the words.

"Of course it did." *More than you'll ever know.* She stifled the emotions threatening to derail her exit. Taking a deep breath, she said, "I hope someday you'll understand."

He followed her into the hallway where her bag waited by the door. She'd packed her things that morning. She turned to face him and stopped herself from reaching out to caress his cheek. His green eyes were dark with unexpressed anger. She couldn't blame him. She'd react the same if their roles were reversed.

This is the last time you're going to see him, Leine. She wanted to leave him with words to remember her by, but came up empty. *It's for the best. He'll be safe. As long as he's alive, I can live with myself.*

"This obsession you have—of justice at any cost—it's going to consume you."

"It already has."

With that, she shouldered her bag and walked out the door into her new life.

And away from the most genuine love she'd ever known.

4

Two hours after the debacle with the Bomb Maker on Tower Bridge, Leine and Art met on the banks of the Thames near the Tate Modern. The wide concrete promenade near the art museum was filled with happy, animated tourists and passersby, lending a light atmosphere to the brisk fall day—in direct contrast to Leine's dark mood. Two little girls dressed in matching coats and knit leggings screamed in delight as their father blew massive soap bubbles in the air, dashing back and forth in an impressive effort to pop each luminous bubble before it landed.

"So we're back to square one." Art gazed out at the Thames. Despite the cold, he wore his jacket open to the weather.

"Worse. Daniel's out of service for the foreseeable future." Leine stared unseeing at the dark brick wall of the museum. The imposing structure seemed to magnify her frustration at the disastrous meeting on the bridge. Daniel had been whisked to the hospital and was currently undergoing surgery to repair the knife wound to his torso. Expected to survive, he'd been the first to volunteer for the initial meeting and was Art's right hand.

Although she was relieved he would recover, his injury was a huge loss in her search for Salome.

"We'll find her."

Leine turned around and leaned on the railing, her gaze moving from the family playing on the quayside to the ship traffic plying the river. "There must be some way to locate her. She can't have just dropped off everyone's radar."

"Have you tried Lou? Maybe he's got some ideas."

"Maybe," Leine replied. She'd have to be careful when she contacted him. She didn't want to chance putting Lou in Salome's crosshairs. "Did you leave anyone at the hospital to keep an eye on Daniel?" she asked. "The Bomb Maker doesn't strike me as a complacent man. He'd want to tie up loose ends."

"I've got two guys there now. One's stationed outside the ER, and the other is roaming. They'll spell each other when Danny's assigned to a room."

"Good." Just then, a river cruise glided by, snippets of running narrative fed through loudspeakers echoing on the light breeze, reminding her of the terrorist attack Salome instigated in Paris months before. She'd used a similar boat on the Seine.

"We need to find Damil."

Art glanced at her. "You mean the guy who helped Salome in Libya?"

"He also set the explosives under the Pont de l'Alma. That tells me she trusts him." Damil had also been Salome's go-to guy when it came to finding suicide bombers.

"You met in Libya?" Art asked.

Leine nodded. "He was shaking down a ten-year-old street kid in an alley in Tripoli. If I hadn't happened along, he and his friend would have killed her." Yet another reason she hadn't contacted Jinn while she was in London. It was safer to leave her be. She also didn't want to disrupt the kid's new life.

Art shook his head and muttered a curse under his breath

that sounded a lot like scum-sucking bastard. "I know a couple of people in Libyan intelligence. If Salome's guy was active around Tripoli I'll bet there's a photograph or two of him. You could circulate the picture with a few people and see if you get a hit."

"That could work." Leine nodded thoughtfully. "I know someone there who owes me a favor. Let me try him first." Paul Miller was a CIA operative who worked out of Tripoli Station and had coordinated the intelligence agencies involved in fighting the terrorist attack in Paris. He'd be able to access the information if it was there. If Paul wasn't comfortable providing additional data on Damil, she'd ask Lou to circulate the photograph. The director for SHEN had contacts in several intelligence circles. Combined with Art's connections, there shouldn't be a problem finding him.

THE NEXT AFTERNOON, LEINE HAD HER PICTURE. PAUL MILLER had sent three. One showed Damil in profile from the waist up. The second was a grainy black and white surveillance video that captured him walking into a train station. The third completed the trifecta, showing his features head on as he went through customs and immigration. Shot from above, the last photograph had more than enough data points for facial recognition software. True to form, Miller had advised Leine that the images would be the extent of his help in the matter due to liability issues he assumed would be triggered by her "interest." Leine encrypted the files and forwarded them to Lou and Art.

If they couldn't come up with a match and weren't able to find Damil, she'd have to figure out a Plan B. Who did she know that might have more information about Salome's whereabouts? Leine racked her brain for someone, anyone who might be willing to help her. Short of infiltrating Izz Al-Din's terrorist network, she was coming up blank.

But there were people she'd worked with at the agency who had gone out on their own. Elite assassins were in demand the world over, either as personal security or freelance hitmen and women. Leine had fielded a few of those job offers herself. She might be able to glean some information from one of them. As long as they wanted to be found.

And there was one person she hadn't tapped yet who might be interested in helping her, although his loyalties weren't always clear.

She pulled out her phone and called her old friend, Spencer Simms.

5

Soho, London

L eine had just finished a simple meal of fresh fish and steamed vegetables in her rented flat in Soho when her phone alerted her to an incoming message. It was from Lou.

Found a match for your photograph.

She opened the attachment and read through the report before leaning back in her chair. Damil was in London. That the two main players in Salome's last bombing attempt were in the same place at the same time could only mean one thing.

She was planning something.

Leine's upcoming meeting with Spencer Simms took on a new level of urgency. He was due in to St. Pancras Station at 6:30 that evening. She checked her watch—she had just enough time to contact Art to tell him about the facial recog match, and to let him know where and when she was meeting Simms.

Like Leine, Simms was a former assassin. Unlike Leine, his loyalties lay wherever the most money could be found. A former colleague at the agency, for the past few years Spencer Simms had been working security for a wealthy French businessman with ties to organized crime. In that capacity, Simms was a walking encyclopedia of European underworld figures. He'd also saved her life.

She just wasn't sure she could trust him.

"RUMOR HAS IT SOME UNSAVORY CHARACTERS FROM LIBYA HAVE been seen lurking about London." Spencer Simms took a sip of his drink and surveyed the bar. The trendy wood- and brass-filled pub near King's Cross where Leine suggested they meet was light-years away from his preferred haunt in a seedy neighborhood in Paris.

He'd just arrived on the Eurostar from Gare du Nord and appeared to have slept most of the way. His thick blond hair stuck up in back, giving him a boyish quality, one he'd exploited in his days as an assassin. He'd seduced more women into giving up their secrets than there were croissants in a French *boulangerie*.

"Anything that could connect it to Salome?" Leine asked.

"Not really. But you know and I know it's a pretty safe bet."

"What's she planning?" Leine mused aloud.

"If it were me, I'd pick up Damil and persuade him to talk."

"That's the plan." Leine pulled up the CCTV picture on her phone and slid it toward him on the bar. "The only problem being that Salome would know someone was onto her. As it is, there are multiple agencies looking for the Bomb Maker for several attacks—I don't know of anyone looking for Damil."

"Use the right leverage and you could have an entrée into her network of thugs. Move on the information quickly enough and she might not get wind of your carefully crafted plans."

"Depends on whether Damil turns against his master. That's a long shot. We don't have enough time to do it right."

"True." Spencer drummed his fingers on the bar as he thought. "Even so, I think Damil is your best bet. You did say he was the nephew of one of your contacts from the old days, right?"

"He was. His uncle is no longer with us." Damil's Uncle Henri had been one of Leine's weapons suppliers in Paris. He was recently deceased, the result of an unfortunate career move on his part.

"Too bad. Would've been good leverage."

"It still might be."

Spencer paused, his drink midway to his lips. "How so?"

"He's aware I was involved in the incident leading up to his uncle being killed. Salome made certain of that."

Spencer lifted his chin. "Ah. Nothing like revenge to motivate a man."

Leine sighed. "Kidnapping him appears to be my best course. Still, I'd prefer something less obvious. Abduction can backfire in a big way."

"Murphy's Law, you mean?" Spencer smiled and finished his drink. "Let me know if you need anything. This vendetta of yours sounds right up my alley."

"It's not a vendetta."

"Oh? Then what would you call hunting down an adversary with the intention of 'neutralizing' her?" He used air quotes around the word neutralizing.

"A public service."

"Is the money good?"

"There's no money."

Simms smiled and shook his head. "You really haven't changed, have you?"

"What do you mean?"

"You were always about justice. Money didn't matter—taking out the bad guys, now, that's what really turned you on."

"Which is why I had to leave the agency."

Simms snorted. "Don't tell me you didn't suspect that weasel Eric was into lining his own pockets."

Leine looked away, her anger rising. Eric, her immediate supervisor at the agency, had been using agency resources to fulfill questionable contracts, which included hiring Leine and her fiancé, Carlos, to eliminate people who weren't deemed threats to national security. When Carlos discovered his scheme, Eric shut him down. Permanently.

She shook off the bitter memory and took a sip of wine. "No, but I found out, didn't I?"

"I'm sorry. I didn't mean to bring up old ghosts."

Leine shrugged. "You're right. I should have known." She'd been idealistic then, assumed everyone around her felt the same way she did. She'd been wrong.

Lesson learned.

Simms took another drink and set the glass on the bar. "Look, I'm in, whatever you decide. Consider it my penance for being a jaded, crusty old assassin who assumed everyone was out for themselves and decided to get my share. Just tell me what you want me to do."

"How do you feel about enhanced interrogation?"

6

Static erupted in Leine's earpiece as she searched the busy boulevard for her objective. Low clouds hung over the posh West London neighborhood, threatening rain. Art Kowalski was once again acting as overwatch and had apparently spotted someone or something nearby.

"Two o'clock. Dark blue hoodie."

Leine glanced down the sidewalk, past the trendy cafés and pubs, searching for the man who could lead her to Salome. A guy in his mid-twenties wearing a navy blue hooded sweatshirt and black jeans walked toward her. White wires sprouted from his ears like anemic spaghetti as he bobbed his head to the music coming through his earphones. Memories surfaced of when she'd first encountered him and another of Salome's henchmen in an alley in Tripoli. The two thugs were about to kill Jinn, a ten-year-old street kid with sticky fingers. For a cell phone. Leine had knocked out Damil and killed the other—the man holding a gun to the child's head.

No lost sleep there. At the time, if she'd known of Damil's role in the attack in Paris she would have eliminated him, too.

But there'd been enough killing that day and she had let him live.

"Got him." Leine zipped her leather jacket closed and adjusted her sunglasses as she waited for Damil to narrow the distance between them. She positioned herself for economy of movement—no point in alerting passersby. She closed her fingers around the grip of the Beretta in her pocket and slid it free, careful to keep it out of sight. The pistol was an effective means to compel him to do as she asked, even though it was the middle of the day and there were too many witnesses—not the best environment for an abduction. She would have to lure him off the main thoroughfare and into a waiting van.

"Easy, now. Don't scare him off." Art's voice echoed in her earpiece.

Damil came abreast of her position. Leine stepped forward, grasped his arm, and poked the barrel of the gun into his ribcage. He stiffened and pulled away, but she kept a tight grip. He yanked out one of his earbuds.

"Do as I say and you live," Leine said in a low voice, her smile intended to diffuse questioning looks from passersby. "Walk." No one appeared to notice the intimate drama playing out on the busy sidewalk.

"What do you want?" Damil said, as she prodded him down a deserted residential side street.

"I knew your uncle, Henri."

Damil swiveled his head, trying to get a good look at her, but Leine shoved the gun hard into his side and he quickly abandoned the attempt.

They walked to an idling white van parked near a row of upscale brick homes. The door slid open, and Zarko jumped out. His tattooed forearms, multiple piercings, and penetrating stare gave him an intimidating look. Damil slowed, obviously anxious about the new addition.

"What's going on? What do you want?" he protested, unease lacing his words.

Leine shoved him forward. Zarko caught him by the shoulders and turned him around, expertly wrapping his wrists with flex cuffs. He patted him down and discovered a knife, a loaded semiauto, and a mobile phone, which he tossed to Leine.

With a quick glance to make sure no one was nearby, he brought out a black fabric hood, which he pulled over Damil's head before he shoved him into the cargo area and slammed the door closed. He then ejected the magazine from Damil's gun, wiped the weapons clean, and dropped the items into a plastic shopping bag.

With a nod at Leine, Zarko moved around the back of the van and got in the driver's side. After a quick scan of the contact list, Leine removed the battery and sim card from Damil's phone before she climbed into the passenger seat and closed the door. A metal cage separated the prisoner from the front seat. Damil sat ramrod straight with his back against the side door.

"That was too easy," Zarko commented as he pulled away from the curb. Leine tossed the battery through the window, hitting the rim of a nearby rubbish bin.

"We caught him by surprise. According to Henri, he was never much of a fighter. More like a thuggish errand boy."

"He's still a terrorist. You can't be too careful, in my opinion."

Leine gave him a sidelong glance. "You think he's bait?"

Zarko shrugged.

"Take us somewhere and check."

A few minutes later, Zarko pulled to the side of a tree-lined park six blocks from the main thoroughfare. There was no pedestrian activity—the small greenspace appeared buttoned up for the day, most likely due to the probability of rain. He exited the vehicle and came around to the side of the van where he slid the door open. Damil turned his head toward him as he climbed inside.

"What are you doing?" Damil's muffled voice had an edge.

"Taking off your shoes."

"I can't breathe." Damil's ragged panting became more pronounced. Zarko lifted the hood.

Leine slid her pistol free and aimed it through the cage at the man's chest. The movement distracted him, and he turned to look at her. Recognition lit Damil's eyes and he sneered.

"You're the bitch who killed my uncle." Hatred sparked from his narrowed gaze and he spit in her direction, missing her by a mile.

"Not exactly," Leine replied. "But I'm not here to argue."

Zarko seized him by the calves and yanked him closer. He proceeded to pry off the well-worn leather boots and then zip-tied his ankles together. Using his own knife, Zarko sliced through the soles and interior until the shoes were shredded. He reached inside his front pocket and pulled out a short black wand. He flicked a switch, creating a low hum. Waving it over the shoes, he checked the readout on the bug detector. "Nothing here." He tossed what was left of the shoes into the corner of the van, then felt the hem of Damil's jeans and hoodie.

"Anything?" Leine asked.

Zarko shook his head. "No." He tugged the hood back down over the prisoner's face.

"Check his arms and legs."

Zarko pushed Damil's sleeves up and ran the wand along his arms, searching for signs of an embedded tracker. He did the same with his calves and feet.

"Nothing. You want me to continue?"

"Yeah."

Salome wasn't someone to be trifled with. Their lives and the life of the prisoner depended on making sure they weren't tracked.

Leine kept the gun trained on Damil as Zarko stripped him to his underwear to search him more thoroughly.

"Nothing."

"Better safe than sorry, right?"

"Yep." Zarko tossed Damil's clothes in a corner and returned to the driver's seat.

Art's voice came through her earpiece. "Well? How'd it go?"

Leine keyed her mic and said, "We've got the package. ETA is —" She glanced at Zarko.

"Thirty minutes, give or take."

"Thirty," Leine confirmed.

"Copy that." Art's tone was all business. "See you then."

7

Thirty-five minutes and several countersurveillance moves later, Leine and Zarko pulled into a garage on a quiet street on the outskirts of London. Leine exited the van and rolled the garage door closed.

Zarko cut the plastic tie around Damil's ankles, and he and Leine marched the prisoner into the house, up a flight of stairs, and through a reinforced steel door which opened onto an empty kitchen. They moved through an archway into a large, barren living room. In the center of the room, a large roll of sheet plastic was visible on the floor next to a wooden chair.

The scuffed and pitted plank floors were worn to a dark patina, and the place smelled of mildew and questionable circumstances. There didn't appear to be any heat in the obviously abandoned building, and the cool fall weather was making its presence known. Narrow, floor-to-ceiling windows stretched across the far wall, covered in thick, dust-filled drapes that did little to alleviate the chill. Even the soundproofing Art added to the walls and ceiling couldn't stop the insidious damp. Lit by a lone floor lamp, the place sported chipped, buff-colored paint covered by dots of black mold.

Art waited for them near a card table positioned several feet from the chair on the plastic. The tanned and fit sixty-five-year-old warrior's alert blue eyes reminded Leine of a hawk's gaze. His close-cropped, steel-gray hair conjured an earlier life in the military. Relaxed but alert, he wore a loose-fitting, dark blue windbreaker over a blue and white plaid flannel shirt, a pair of jeans, and black crepe-soled shoes.

She'd worked with Art during a tense rescue operation in Greece the year before, and she'd come to trust him and his team. His long experience as a personal protection operator and several years as a member of foreign intelligence active in Libya, Iraq, and Afghanistan made Art uniquely qualified to locate people who didn't want to be found. If it hadn't been for him and his team, the delicate balance of power in a tense geopolitical conflict would have been destroyed, leading to war.

Another of Art's guys stood off to the side, his arms crossed. He went by the name of Jorge and wore similar attire to Art's. His shaved head accentuated a tattoo of the Rod of Asclepius running up his neck. The team medic, Jorge was an immensely effective operative, and both Leine and Zarko had worked with him on the operation in Greece.

Zarko led Damil, hooded and still clad in only his underwear, to the lone wooden chair across from Art and sat him down. He secured the prisoner's arms and legs to the chair with tape, yanked the hood off, and tossed it on the card table. Damil squinted in the dusty beam of light cast by the floor lamp. An involuntary shiver racked his shoulders.

Leine walked over to a canvas bag on the floor next to the table and pulled out a metal box. Three plastic-coated wires with alligator clips on each end trailed from one side with a set of controls and a blank digital readout on the other. She set the box on top of the table and uncoiled the attached power cord, which she connected to a power bank already set up on the floor. The readout blinked red several times before settling on zero.

Damil watched all this with increasing alarm, his eyes growing ever larger as the import of her actions began to sink in.

Exactly what Leine intended. She leveled her gaze at him.

"What are you going to do with that?" he asked her, nodding at the device. His voice rang hollow in the empty space. Despite the chill in the room, tiny beads of sweat appeared on his forehead.

"That's up to you." Leine picked up the three long wires and separated them, checking each clip. Then she fiddled with the knob until the box emitted a low hum. She reached into the bag and brought out a metal screwdriver with a rubber grip and touched the end to one of the clips. The surfaces arced and popped.

Damil's gaze was riveted to the metal box. Leine put the screwdriver down and stepped toward him. He tore his gaze from the electrical device, his breath quick and shallow.

"It should be me who is questioning you," he said, his voice thick with false bravado.

Leine raised an eyebrow. "Oh? How do you figure that?"

"After years of working with him, you killed my uncle. Why?"

"I didn't actually kill him."

"Liar."

"Didn't he tell you? Your uncle set me up. He told your employer where and who I was and she agreed to fund a contract."

"Liar!" Damil said again. "He would never have betrayed a friend."

Leine almost felt sorry for the guy. Almost.

"I hate to break it to you, Damil, but Henri was all about the booty—both in business and pleasure." The woman he'd selected to kill her had been a protégé of Henri's, although Leine was pretty sure he had hoped to get the twenty-something into bed. Of course, the bounty Salome put on Leine's head after Henri revealed that Leine was the notorious assassin known as the Leopard might have had something to do with his betrayal.

Luckily, his attempt failed. When Leine confronted him, his security force made the mistake of trying to neutralize her. One of the rounds meant for her found a home in Henri. Leine couldn't say she was sad it happened, although he had been a damn good arms dealer.

Leine shrugged. "Believe what you want. How do you think I got your name? Your precious uncle gave you up faster than you can say 'family.' It's not like Salome called and told me who you were."

Doubt shadowed his features for a moment but was quickly replaced by his default bluster. "What do you want?"

"I want to know where your employer is."

"I don't know what you are talking about."

Leine nodded at Zarko, who picked up two wires and advanced toward him, snapping the clips together like tiny dinosaur teeth.

"I think you do."

Damil's lips hardened into a straight line and he glared at Leine. "I will not tell you *anything*."

"Yes, you will. Everybody breaks—at some point. It just depends on how much you're willing to endure for the cause." Leine would have preferred a more finessed interrogation, but Art had argued that the longer it took to draw the information out of him, the less coherent or reliable his answers were likely to be. Reluctantly, Leine had agreed.

"How did you find me?"

He was playing for time. Leine wasn't about to tell him that Spencer Simms followed him from the pub he frequented for lunch to his flat in an upscale neighborhood in West London. Routine was an operative's Achilles heel. He should have known that.

Zarko squeezed one of the clips open and lowered it toward his left pectoral muscle. "This is going to hurt." He clamped the little metal teeth onto his nipple and Damil drew in a sharp breath. Squeezing his eyes shut, he took several deep breaths. Zarko connected the second clip to his other nipple and stepped away.

"Hold on a minute," Leine said. "I almost forgot." She nodded at the roll of plastic beside the chair. Zarko grabbed one end, unrolled a large section, and then slid it across the floor in front of Damil.

"Body fluids have a tendency to spray out during this kind of questioning," she said as Zarko rocked Damil's chair back on two legs and tucked the plastic underneath. "Things can get a little messy."

"Oh, yeah," Art said. "Remember when that guy's testicle exploded? Better make sure it's covering a wide enough area."

Zarko nodded as he tugged the plastic under the back of the chair. "Like the lady said, messy." Damil stared straight ahead, his jaw clenched.

Leine signaled Art, and he fiddled with the dial on the metal box.

"Make it count," she said.

As soon as the current reached the clips, Damil's body went rigid and his fingers curled around the armrests. Art let the machine do its job before cutting the power several seconds later. Damil hung his head and slumped back in the chair.

Not waiting for him to recover, Leine asked, "Where is she?"

"I told you I don't know who you are talking about," he wheezed.

Leine sighed. "Okay. If that's the way you want to play it."

She twirled her finger in the air, giving Art the go-ahead to continue.

The second time wasn't as gentle, although could be tolerated by someone Damil's age and size. Earlier, when they were planning the abduction, she and Art had decided how much to increase the current each time based on a healthy twenty-five-year-old male, then added their previous experiences to the mix. Leine had been subject to a similar ordeal back in her assassin days, and she knew well the excruciating jolt of electricity that barreled through such a sensitive area.

Damil tried not to scream, but the current was too much and he wailed in agony. Art cut the juice, and the prisoner collapsed against the chair, gasping.

"You're lucky," Leine said. "When I got to experience this little exercise, I was soaked to the skin and hanging by my arms from a chain on a freezing cold trawler."

The prisoner whimpered through shallow breaths. Leine stepped closer. She grabbed his chin and brought his head up so she could look him in the eyes.

"Where is she?"

Pain and misery were obvious in his gaze, but so was something else. Resignation flickered in the depths. It wouldn't be long now.

Damil shook his head. "I—can't. If I tell you she will kill me," he whispered.

Leine bent down close and in a quiet voice said, "We'll kill you if you don't." She waited, allowing him room to reach the only conclusion he could. When he hesitated, she glanced at Zarko. "You're going to have to connect the third one."

Grimacing, Zarko picked up the third wire and walked over to Damil. He opened the clip and reached for his crotch.

"No—wait." The prisoner closed his eyes and shuddered. He took a deep breath. "She has changed her appearance."

"How?"

"Her nose and chin."

The reconstructive surgery wasn't a surprise. Facial recognition was hard to avoid, especially in airports and train stations. Salome might have found some wealthy backers who could provide a private jet or possibly a boat, but at some point if she was on the move, she'd have to appear in public. CCTV cameras were ubiquitous, especially in European cities and airports, not to mention the borders.

"Why are there so many of your compatriots in London? What's she planning?"

Damil shook his head. "I don't know. I just know what she told me."

"And what was that?"

"To meet her in London. She rented me an apartment."

"What else? Where is she now?"

Damil shook his head. "She's never in one place for long. She's—how do you say it? Paranoid."

That was good. Paranoid people often made mistakes. The details of trying to stay ahead of perceived surveillance got to be too much. Stressed people were usually careless people.

"Where was she the last time you spoke?"

"Brussels. She was going to—"

There was a sharp *crack!* from the window at the far end of the room, and Damil's head snapped backward, exploding into a spray of blood and bits of brain and bone.

"*Sniper!*" Leine shouted, and dove for cover.

8

T hree more rounds sliced through the curtains and chewed up the floor where Leine had been standing just seconds before.

Pulling the Beretta from its holster, she sprinted to the kitchen while Art, Jorge, and Zarko scrambled for cover.

Abruptly, the shooting stopped. In the eerie aftermath, the only sounds echoing in the empty flat were the team's ragged breathing and the relentless drip of Damil's blood onto the black plastic sheet. Heart pounding, Leine moved to the kitchen window and eased two blinds apart with the tip of the Beretta. There was no sign of the shooter.

"Find him," Art growled. Zarko cracked the door to the apartment and checked to make sure no one was there before he and Jorge disappeared down the stairwell. "Goddammit. Did you check him for a tracker?"

Leine nodded. "There was nothing on him."

"What about his gun?"

"We tossed everything on our way here."

Art grimaced. "How the hell did Salome manage to find us?"

Leine glanced back through the archway at what was left of

the prisoner's head. "The shooter must have had a thermal scope."

"That would explain the precision hit through a curtained window."

"Yeah."

"Jorge and I got here an hour before you and Zarko showed up. I had him case the building across the street. He cleared everywhere a sniper would set up, including the roof and an empty apartment on one of the upper floors."

"You and Jorge have worked together a long time. I assume you can be sure he wasn't compromised?"

Art nodded. "I did everything I know to make certain we weren't followed, but Salome could have had either or both of us under surveillance. Maybe she had more guys in place at the bridge than we initially confirmed."

"That still doesn't explain how she knew you and Jorge were involved. This isn't a lucky guess. I made it a point not to use anyone tied to Paris. She could have gotten information on the security firm I worked with from the news coverage. Finding out about you would have been much more difficult since she didn't know you were involved in the Sakharov operation. This could have been her smoking us out."

"Possible." Art eased the door to the stairwell open and peered into the murky darkness. "You need to get out of here." He nodded and they descended to the ground floor, guns drawn. Art led her to the rear exit of the building. He cracked the door open and checked the long, narrow yard.

"You guys find anything?" Art said into his mic.

There was a slight delay before Jorge answered. "Nothing. The apartment I checked earlier is still empty, but one of the windows was open."

"Shit." Art eyed Leine and shook his head.

"We missed something. A locator device, something." Leine

ran through different scenarios leading up to Damil's capture. How did Salome find them?

"I thought you said Zarko tore everything apart."

"He did. Let's split up," Leine suggested. "I'll meet you at the third alternate in two hours." The third alternate was a small pub in Soho, near a neighborhood park. A certain bench there also served as a dead drop for messages to and from Lou Stokes, the director for SHEN.

"Roger that. I'll tidy up here. Be safe."

Leine holstered her gun and tucked her hair under the knit cap she'd stuffed in her coat pocket. She slid on a pair of sunglasses before she exited the building and turned left, heading off down the narrow alley.

For what seemed like the umpteenth time since she set out to find Salome, the operation had gone sideways, but she'd survived.

Now, all bets were off.

AN HOUR AND A HALF LATER, LEINE ARRIVED AT THE DESIGNATED park bench and checked under the seat. Nothing. Leine surreptitiously taped an encrypted note for Lou in a spot underneath at the back of the bench, letting him know she would be contacting him later that evening.

She glanced at the pub across the expanse of lawn that Art and she had designated as their third meeting spot. The first was near the Thames in East London, and was reserved for when they had to leave the city quickly via boat. The second was a small café near St. Pancras railway station.

Art was making his way along the street toward the pub. Leine checked to make sure he hadn't been followed before she went to meet him.

"So what's our next move?" Art asked once they'd found an empty table inside the historic brick building. The space was cozy, dark, and anonymous—the perfect place to meet. They both ordered a pint.

"She knows someone's trying to find her. Otherwise, she wouldn't have tracked Damil." Leine took a long pull on her beer and set the glass on the table.

"Yeah, but the real question is, does she know who we are?"

"I'm proceeding as though she does. Have your guys lay low for a few days. Maybe head to Amsterdam for some R&R. I'll call you with a new plan by Friday."

"Will do. You're giving up on London?"

"No. But she won't be easy to find if she's here. Not when she knows she's being hunted."

Leine sighed and stared out the window. A light drizzle had begun to fall, casting everything in bleak battleship gray. It corresponded perfectly with Leine's current mood.

"I need some time to think," she said. "Contact me when you and your team get settled."

"Have you checked with Simms?"

Leine shook her head. "Not yet. I'll call him after I leave, see if he has any brilliant ideas."

"I'll rattle some cages, try to get something to shake loose."

"I'd appreciate it."

"Not a problem." Art nodded. "Hey, this was just a minor setback. Nobody on our team died. We'll find her."

"I hope it's before she puts in motion whatever she's planning." She drained her glass.

"Amen." Art ordered bangers and mash and a glass of bourbon. Leine drained her glass and got up to leave. He looked a question at her.

"Not hungry."

Art waved her off. "Be careful out there," he said.

She walked out the door into the lightly falling rain and checked her watch. She'd give Spencer Simms a call, but first she'd try contacting Anatoly Sakharov—a man who had direct experience with Salome when she was an assassin. It was worth a shot.

With a slight shiver, she zipped her jacket against the rain and headed back to her flat.

9

"Damil's dead."

"Good." Salome flipped through the photographs on her phone showing what the assassin described as a cleanup crew hoisting something covered in black plastic into a waiting van with a home repair logo on the side. One of the shots was of a man with close-cropped gray hair and bright blue eyes who appeared to be overseeing the operation.

"Who is the older man?" she asked.

"I don't know his name," the assassin replied. Salome had him on speaker so she could look at the photos. "He was waiting for the cleanup crew and let them inside the building. He was also part of Damil's welcoming committee."

Salome continued on to the next picture. Her breath caught as she stared at the profile of a woman with dark hair and sunglasses. She'd recognize that face anywhere. *Leine Basso.* So it *was* her. She swiped to the next image, which showed a heavily tattooed man shoving Damil into the back of a white van.

"The woman." She flipped back to Basso's picture. "She was involved?"

"She intercepted Damil and led him to the van."

The appearance of the Basso woman compressed her time-line considerably. Although she knew the former assassin was searching for her, she hadn't been aware how close she was until now. Salome no longer had the luxury of time, a loss that would have its own consequences. "I have more work for you, if you're interested."

"That would depend on certain things," the man answered.

"Yes, you've made it very clear that money is your main concern. You'll be paid well, I assure you." The man's familiarity with Basso alone was worth his steep price. Add to that his status as a premier assassin, and she'd gladly pay double.

"When can I expect the final payment for the Damil job?" he asked.

"The money will be in your account by close of business today." She checked the time. The Bomb Maker would be arriving shortly. "As for the next job, someone will contact you." She ended the call.

Damil's loss was a setback, but not one that would hamper her strategy. He was a pawn in a high-level chess match—the sacrifice was worthwhile. He was but one option to lure Leine Basso into the open.

After the fiasco in Paris, Salome had assumed the Basso woman would be searching for her and took evasive steps. She altered her appearance enough so that she could come and go without an exact match in all but the most finely tuned facial recognition databases. Her recovery time from the plastic surgery was spent at a luxury spa in the south of France planning how to get back in the Kremlin's good graces, as well as how she could eliminate Leine Basso for good. She'd enlisted the help of an old friend—an oligarch who enjoyed unprecedented access to the Russian president—and had alerted several contacts in the criminal underworld that had an axe to grind, either with the US or Basso herself. Salome rubbed her new chin absentmindedly, thinking about her next move. Everything had to be executed in perfect order, or she would again fall short of her objective.

She couldn't allow that to happen.

Salome accessed her contacts and dialed another number. When the person at the other end picked up she said, "Tell our mutual friend it is time."

10

H eather Brody sipped her beer and looked at the screen on her phone. Seven twenty-five. She'd told Santa seven thirty at the Rusty Scupper. She brushed a lock of freshly washed hair behind her ear, glad she had time for a couple of pre-date drinks before the meeting with her partner. Her nerves frayed because of her plan, she'd gone surfing that afternoon. Surfing always calmed her down. Put her in the zone.

But her nerves were sneaking up on her again. Hence the extra alcohol.

Stop it, Brody. Everything's going to be fine.

The Rusty Scupper was an old surfer bar near the beach. The ancient, wide-plank flooring held the scuffs and scrapes of a thousand and one epic evenings, and the pool table near the back had the stains to prove it. Salt and sand filled the hard-to-sweep corners and lent a certain authenticity to the place. The owner, an old surfer of some renown, liked it that way. Heather felt more at home there than in her own living room. Probably not the best place for a homicide detective to spend her free time, but then again, Heather had never been conventional.

She'd been ecstatic when she'd been promoted to the coveted detective position in the elite robbery-homicide division of the LAPD, or RHD as it was known within the department. Predictably, the advancement elevated her status with some of the rank and file, and marked her as a "token woman hire" with others, namely among division detectives with more time on the job.

All that faded when held up to the bright light of her achievements solving high-profile murders for the Los Angeles Police Department. An accomplished surfer, she also volunteered her time with disadvantaged youth by teaching them to ride the waves, and helped out in a local soup kitchen that catered to the homeless near a favorite beach. She played a mean game of volleyball and could hold her own on the banjo.

The door to the bar opened and Santiago Jensen walked in. Heather caught herself staring at his smoldering good looks and mentally berated herself. He was used to women coming on to him, had turned down every one of them since he'd started seeing Leine Basso. She respected that about him.

But he was a free man now. All bets were off.

Heather shifted on the barstool and hiked her skirt a little higher to show more of her muscular and perfectly tanned leg. That was one thing about surfing that never let her down—if she went out every day, her body stayed as fit as if she were nineteen.

She waved him over. He gave her a nod as he threaded his way through the mismatched tables and chairs. Her heart thudded in her chest, and she took a deep breath to calm herself. Ever since she'd been assigned as his partner, she'd fantasized about what he was like in bed. Unlike most of the other detectives in the division, he was in fantastic shape and always had a kind word for anyone. Lately, though, his mood had taken a darker turn, and she'd been concerned. She asked him what was wrong, but true to form Santa had told her it was nothing and not to worry. That was when Carol in dispatch confirmed the rumor that he and Leine had broken up.

Tonight, Heather Brody was going to help him out of his bad mood. And hopefully out of his jeans and *Gimme Shelter* T-shirt.

"Nice place," he said, perusing the kitschy décor of fishnets and glass floats hanging from the ceiling. To add more interest, there were several shellacked and bloated puffer fish suspended from fishing line and a surfboard with a chunk missing, purportedly involved in an attack by a Great White.

"What are you having?" Heather asked, signaling the bartender.

"Dos Equis."

"Coming right up, brah." The bartender reached into a cooler under the counter and set the bottle of beer on the bar.

Santa reached for his wallet but Heather put her hand on his arm. "I've got it." She handed the bartender a twenty. "Santiago Jensen, meet Mikey," she said, introducing the two men.

Santa and Mikey shook hands. "Good to meet ya," Mikey said, smiling. Heather loved his Australian accent and wicked sense of humor—she could listen to him for hours. He made change and then left to take care of another patron.

"You don't have to do that, you know." Santa smiled and had a seat on the stool next to her.

Heather shrugged. "I asked you here, remember? The least I can do is pay for your drink."

He lifted the beer in a salute before taking a swig. "Here's to you."

Heather clinked bottles with him and took a drink herself. The cold beer slid down her dry throat, lending her additional courage.

"So what exactly is this about?" he asked.

"Can't a girl have a drink with her partner?"

Santa shrugged. "I'm just surprised. You never asked before."

She wanted to say, *you were never available before,* but decided against it. *Let the night unfold the way it's meant to,* she thought.

"I figured it was high time to get to know the real Santiago Jensen." She waved Mikey over and ordered two shots of tequila. Things needed to move along a little faster, or she'd lose her nerve. She circled her finger in the air, telling Mikey to keep them coming.

"Not much to know."

"Oh, now that's just being modest." Heather threw back the shot and sucked on a wedge of lime. Santa did the same. "Apparently you've forgotten how many cases you've solved."

"It's my job. Besides, you know that part."

"I also know that you love kite surfing and rock and roll."

"Okay. What's this really about?" He slid his phone onto the bar, checking the screen as he did.

Shit. I lost him already. Mikey set two more shots in front of them. Heather downed hers immediately. It was the good stuff—smooth with a velvety aftertaste. There wasn't the burn like with cheap tequila. Ignoring his, Santa sipped his beer and eyed the baseball game playing on the flat screen above the bar.

The tequila was beginning to work like it always did. A warm feeling hovered around her, masking the anxiety of what she was about to do. The hangover would be so worth it if it involved waking up next to Santa.

"Looks like I'm ahead of you," she said, nodding at the shot glass in front of him.

"Tomorrow's a work day. I've never been a fan of solving cases hungover."

He smiled as he spoke, but Heather got the impression he was dead serious. She smiled back and leaned in closer. "I know, but we've both been working so hard, I thought maybe we could let our hair down a little." She gave him a sultry look that always, one hundred percent, worked on anyone she set her sights on.

Not this time.

Santa drained his beer and moved to stand. Heather grabbed his arm, and he hesitated. With a sigh, he sat back down.

"What am I doing here?" he asked.

It's now or never, Brody. "I—ah, I heard about you and Leine," she began.

Something swept across his eyes, so quickly that she couldn't catch what the emotion might be. Then it was gone as if someone had rolled a heavy door down, closing off all access.

"Yeah, and?"

"And I thought maybe you could use a shoulder to cry on." *Or a body to make love to,* she silently added.

Santa nodded in understanding. "Well, thanks, but I'm doing all right. Really."

Emboldened by his acceptance of her explanation, she decided to go a step further. "Do you mind if I ask what happened? You two seemed so happy."

The emotion floated across his face once more, and this time he didn't bother to hide it. It was a mixture of sadness and bewilderment.

"We were. It was just—bad timing." He signaled Mikey to bring him another beer, which he did.

"I'm sorry. Breakups are never easy."

A smile played on his lips. "And you would know that, how?"

Heather grinned. "Well, I've heard, anyway." They both laughed. *Yeah, this is the way the night should be going.* Relieved, she pointed to her empty shot glass. "I'm going to order another. Join me?"

"Okay. But that's it."

An hour later, they were laughing about an old murder case

of Santa's that went sideways for the murderer when he showed up drunk at the station and confessed.

"Easiest case I ever worked," he said, smiling.

"If only all of them could be that simple." Heather sighed wistfully. She leaned her head on her hand in an effort to maintain. She'd had a couple more shots—or was it three?—and was having a hard time focusing.

"I think we'd better call it a night." Santa paid for their drinks and stood.

Heather slid off the barstool and lost her balance, falling toward Santa. He grabbed her by the shoulders to steady her, but she relaxed into him with a giggle.

"I think you've had one too many."

"No kidding." Another giggle escaped her at the feel of his hard chest against her back. *My God, he's so sexy. Just wait 'til I get you in bed, Mr. Man...*

"Did you drive here?"

Heather nodded and pointed toward the door. "In the parking lot."

Santa grabbed her purse. "I'll drive you home. You can catch a ride tomorrow morning to pick up your car."

With his hand on her arm, Santa guided her out of the bar and over to his black 1969 Camaro SS.

"I *love* your ride," Heather said. She giggled to herself. *And I'd love to ride you, Mr. Santa man.*

Still holding her arm, he unlocked the passenger door and opened it wide. "Your chariot awaits, m'lady."

It's now or never. She nestled closer to him and slid her hands up the sides of his face, gripped the back of his head, and brought him down for a kiss. Her gesture met more resistance than she was prepared for. Confused, she pulled back.

"What'sa matter?" she asked.

Santa took hold of her wrists and gently pulled them free. "You need to stop, Heather."

"Why?" was all she could think to say. "We were getting along so well—"

He guided her into the passenger seat and said, "For one, you've had a lot to drink. I'd never take advantage. And two, we're partners. Partners are off limits."

Heather didn't say anything as he closed the door and walked around the back of the car to the driver's side. Off limits? Shit. That meant everything she did that evening wouldn't have worked, no matter what. Or was it that he didn't find her attractive enough? She thought about Leine Basso—gorgeous, shoulder-length dark hair with those shimmery red highlights, tits to die for—she'd bet they were real, too—and long, lean legs. But Heather figured she had her beat by a mile: she was younger, blonder, tanner, and worked with him every day.

Maybe she was too perky. Leine seemed quiet, almost moody. No, not really moody. More like a woman who knew her strengths and wouldn't take shit from anyone. Definitely a badass. Heather had thought she was, too, what with being a detective for the LAPD and an accomplished surfer. That was before she met Leine.

Santa climbed into the driver's seat and started the engine.

"Don't you think I'm attractive?" She had to know.

He sighed as he pulled out of the parking lot. "Like I said, you're my partner. Off limits. Now where do you live?" His tone was more clipped than she remembered it ever being.

She'd fucked up, obviously. Now things would be weird between them. *Shit, Brody. What have you done?* Her cheeks flamed hot as the first blush of humiliation set in.

He didn't say anything, and Heather didn't attempt conversation. Obviously he wasn't in the mood to chitchat. *He wasn't ready yet. Brody, you totally blew it—you were too freaking eager.*

Back in the far recesses of her brain, the idea that she was going to be mortally embarrassed come morning wove its weedy little talons through her mind. Her mood bleak, she stared out the window. *Damned tequila. Damned timing.*

Damned Basso.

11

"The Bomb Maker's been spotted in Edinburgh." Spencer Simms took the seat next to Leine. They were riding the London Underground, better known as the Tube. A woman's voice came over the PA system announcing the next stop.

The brightly lit subway car juddered along, efficiently carrying passengers from one end of London to the other. Leine wasn't headed anywhere in particular, preferring the anonymity of mass transportation and the ability to see if she or Simms were being followed.

It had been four days since the shooting. Simms had volunteered to remain in London and was working his contacts there. Art and his guys were getting some rest in Amsterdam, although Art had feelers out for anything regarding Salome or an imminent terrorist attack. So far, nothing. Lou was searching as well but had come up blank.

Obviously, Salome had gone to ground after Damil's murder.

Her attempts to contact Anatoly Sakharov hadn't been successful. The reclusive billionaire was apparently off the grid. None of his assistants were able to tell her when he'd be back.

The phone number Sakharov had given her after rescuing his daughter in Greece went unanswered.

The Bomb Maker was their best lead in the hunt for Salome.

"Anyone else with him in Edinburgh?" she asked.

"He appears to be flying solo. My source tailed him to a hotel near the Grassmarket."

"How long has he been there?"

"Three days."

"Think it's worth a trip?"

"I'd be up for Edinburgh. I need to top up my whisky cellar."

Leine gave him a look. "What makes you think I want company?"

Simms shrugged. "I figure you can always use someone to watch your back."

"It's not my back I'm worried about," she muttered. The woman's voice came over the loudspeaker again, announcing the next stop. "Text me the address. I'll be in touch." Leine rose and held on to the chrome upright as the train car pulled into the station.

She exited the car with the stream of passengers as a disembodied voice intoned "Mind the gap." She followed the signs out of the station and onto the busy street. Steel gray clouds scudded across an intermittently blue sky, and a cold breeze skated past her. Leine zipped her jacket closed and set off in search of a café.

Why Edinburgh? The obvious explanation was that Salome had moved her team to another city because of Damil's abduction. If so, Leine supposed Edinburgh was as good a place as any. The people were generally quite friendly, and although the city was located far to the north, access to transportation was good.

Not normally known for harboring terrorists, the medieval Grassmarket area where the Bomb Maker had been seen was a

rabbit warren of alleyways and graveyards, lending it a myste-
rious atmosphere.

Salome could have chosen worse. Using her phone, Leine
booked a flight for that afternoon. She didn't have a plan, but
she'd figure one out.

She was tempted to call Art and tell him to meet her there
with a couple of his guys, but didn't want to mobilize the team
with no plan in place. Still, getting Art's read on the situation
might come in handy. He was a good tactician, and they'd
worked well together in Greece.

Leine found a small café and ordered ginger cake with
caramel sauce and a double shot of espresso.

Choosing a window seat with a view of the door, she sat
down and called. Art answered on the second ring.

"I was wondering when you were going to call." Art's voice
sounded like gravel scraping asphalt. Too many cigarettes and
too much booze. Well, that's what R&R was for, wasn't it?

"Having fun?" she asked. Amsterdam was a great place to let
off steam. She figured he and his guys could use the downtime.

Art chuckled. "Those young bucks amaze me at their
capacity for alcohol and women. They leave me in the dust."

Leine snorted. "Whatever you say, Art. I've seen you in
action, and I'm pretty sure none of your guys would be able to
outgun you in anything. Especially the ladies."

"With the exception of Zarko, you mean." The stories of
Zarko's prowess were legendary, belying his surprisingly humble
demeanor.

"Good point. Have you heard anything from Daniel? How's
his recovery?"

"He's doing fine. They moved him to a secure facility, compliments of the company he freelances for. Which puts the two
guys who were guarding him back in action."

"That's good news."

"I assume you didn't call me just to chat. What's up?"

"Our guy's in Edinburgh."

"Who's your source?"

"Spencer Simms."

"And you trust him? I mean, the Damil thing didn't go as planned and he *was* part of it."

"I trust him about as much as I trust anyone in the business. I've got a message in to Lou to let him know I'm headed there. I've booked a flight for later this afternoon."

"What's the plan?"

"That's just it. I don't have one. I figure I'll play things by ear."

There was a brief pause. "Can't say I agree with your tactics. Winging it generally doesn't end well."

"Maybe not for you, but I've had good luck being open when events on the ground are fluid."

"Yeah, but you need a framework to judge that fluidity against."

"What do you propose?"

"Where's he been spotted?"

"Grassmarket, in the old town."

"So lots of tourists, squirrelly alleys, shit like that?"

"Yep."

"I can meet you later tonight or tomorrow—I'll walk around, get a feel for the place. Then, if the target's still there, we can plan our next move."

"My gut tells me we don't have a lot of time. We lose him, and it's possible he doesn't surface again for a while. If Salome's planning something, we need to be there ASAP so we can punch a hole in her plans."

"Okay. How about we each do what we're good at? My team will do recon, and you follow your gut. Both will work. We just need to stay in touch."

"Sounds good. I'll text you the number for my new phone."

SPENCER SIMMS DONNED A DARK KNIT CAP AND PAIR OF BLACK-rimmed glasses before getting off the train at Leicester Square. Tourists crawled through the streets of Picadilly like ants, making anonymity easy. He walked through the square, across the street, and into a restaurant near one of the theaters. Removing his coat, he slid into a booth next to a window and ordered a pint.

A few minutes later, a man in a dark gray overcoat walked in and made his way to where Simms was sitting. He shrugged off his coat and hung it across the back of his seat before he sat down across from him. He wore a burgundy sweater vest over a tan plaid button-down shirt and dark slacks. His round spectacles gave him the appearance of an accountant, which was good in his line of work. Simms couldn't be one hundred percent sure, but the perfectly trimmed goatee looked fake.

"Any news?" the Accountant asked.

"She's on her way to Edinburgh."

He nodded. "I'll pass it along."

"I offered to accompany her as protection."

The Accountant smirked. "I'm sure she appreciated the gesture."

Simms smiled. "Not exactly."

The man checked his phone. "The next flight leaves in two hours. We expect you to be on it."

Simms nodded. "When will I see the money?"

"Soon. There's one more bridge to cross."

"If that money doesn't hit my bank account by the time I check in to my hotel in Edinburgh, you can kiss my ass goodbye."

The Accountant waved away his concerns. "The money's no problem."

Simms narrowed his eyes. "I've heard that song before. There'll be no more meetings until I have confirmation. I'm risking too much to be strung along."

The Accountant removed his glasses and held Spencer Simms's gaze. "Don't worry." He leaned back in the booth as he slid a cloth from his pocket and began to polish the lenses of his glasses. "All in good time."

12

Leine paid the taxi driver and climbed from the cab into the cool, fresh air. Edinburgh was still one of her favorite cities. From the striking 200-foot spire tribute to the poet and writer Sir Walter Scott to the imposing Edinburgh Castle, the city was steeped in history and Scottish pride. Several years before, Leine had laid low in Scotland after a particularly hazardous job for the agency. She'd enjoyed walking the streets of the city at night, getting a feel for what it must have been like to live in medieval Europe. She'd also developed a taste for whisky while she was there. It was hard not to, just as it was hard not to like the Scots. Outspoken and witty was an understatement.

Leine checked into her hotel and took the lift to her room. A bottle of whisky and a dozen blood-red roses waited for her, with a card from Spencer Simms that read, *I'm here if you need me.* He'd added a phone number, written in simple code. She didn't have to wonder how he found her so quickly. He'd have narrowed the list of hotels to the neighborhood where the Bomb Maker was allegedly staying, and he most likely remembered several of her aliases from their work together. Had she used one from the old days? She couldn't recall. Leine made a mental note to have Lou change her passports.

She memorized Simms's number before she burned the card in the bathroom and flushed it down the toilet, and then went to the window. Her room had a solid view of the neighborhood. Taking out the new burner phone she'd purchased on her way to the hotel, she accessed an encrypted messaging system and texted Art and Lou her new number. She'd kept her old phone in case Sakharov called, but she wouldn't use it for this phase of the mission.

She pulled a pair of binoculars from her bag and scanned the streets below, familiarizing herself with the area.

Buildings from the seventeenth and eighteenth centuries marched along the main thoroughfare and up Victoria Street, lending a brooding, historic air to the neighborhood. Students and tourists made up the majority of pedestrians, many there to soak up the square's grisly history of executions, adding a macabre party atmosphere. Case in point: The Last Drop Tavern commemorated the last public hanging in Grassmarket to take place there in the 1700s.

After freshening up, Leine put on a dark gray woolen scarf and cap and a pair of dark glasses, then zipped her leather jacket closed before taking the lift back to the lobby to do her own reconnaissance.

The weather was cooler than in London, with a blustery breeze and dark, foreboding skies. Ruddy-cheeked passersby leaned into the wind, their jackets and coats closed against the chill. Leine walked the winding streets, noting chokepoints and escape routes, then stopped at a small sporting goods shop and purchased a hunting knife and a sheath, which she slid into her waistband. Realizing she hadn't eaten since breakfast, she took a detour and found a small pub for dinner and a drink.

The bartender looked to be in his early twenties. Leine smiled at his eagerness to please.

"Have you worked here long?" she asked.

He bobbed his head as he poured her a pint. "Yeah, since I started university."

"Ever seen this guy?" Leine slid a grainy surveillance photograph of the Bomb Maker across the bar.

The bartender frowned and studied the picture. "He dunna look familiar."

"You'd remember. He's tall and thin with gray eyes, and has a Middle Eastern accent."

He leaned closer, a conspiratorial grin on his face. "What's he, a terrorist or something?" he asked in a loud whisper.

Leine smiled. "Something like that."

"Can't say as I've seen 'im. And I'm here a lot."

"No worries." She grabbed a napkin from the bar, wrote her phone number on it, and slid it toward him. "If you do, would you give me a call? There's some cash in it for you. My name is Gretchen, by the way. I'm staying nearby."

"Robbie." He extended his hand, which Leine shook. "If there's cash involved you can count me in." Robbie smiled and cocked his head. "You wouldn't be looking for a cheap tour guide to the wonders of Edinburgh, now would you?"

It was Leine's turn to smile. "Afraid not. I'm here on business and booked for my entire stay. But thanks for the offer. I'll definitely keep you in mind next time I'm in town." Her waitress walked by with her order, so she picked up her beer and made her way through the crowd to her table.

After dinner, she walked a jagged circuit along Candlemaker Row, past Greyfriars Church and its historic graveyard, and then back to Victoria Street, near where the Bomb Maker was supposed to be staying. Darkness and a faint mist had descended on the city, lending an eerie backdrop to her recon.

The scent of fried fish and salty sea air mingled with cigarette smoke from patrons standing outside the line of pubs near the square.

She staked out the Bomb Maker's hotel's front entrance for a couple of hours but eventually grew restless. She checked her phone. It was after eleven. Deciding to call it a night, she headed back to her room, making sure to choose random streets in case she'd picked up a tail. Doubtful, since no one except Lou, Art, and Spencer Simms knew she was in town.

As she neared her hotel, she noted a shadow in her periphery and changed course, heading down a dark alley. She slid the hunting knife free and, keeping to the shadows, ducked into a dark doorway to wait.

The unmistakable scrape of leather soles on cobblestone echoed toward her. Clinking plates and glasses from a nearby restaurant momentarily drowned out the sound of footsteps, and she strained to listen. Seconds later, a man in a dark coat and fisherman's cap pulled low strode past, hands stuffed in his pockets, his shoulders hunched against the cold. Whoever it was hadn't seen her.

Leine allowed him a long leash before following.

The man reached the end of the alley and hesitated, looking both ways. Leine slowed and considered what to do. Confrontation could go either way, depending on what kind of weapon he carried, but continuing to follow him had its risks, too. Alternatively, he might be an innocent bystander on his way home after a long day.

The man turned right. Leine crossed to the other side of the street and followed. Halfway down the block, he stopped. She slowed and brought out her phone, pretending to text as she walked. When he turned, she bowed her head so her face was cast in shadow. He waited a moment before he turned and resumed his journey.

Leine continued to tail him, always keeping him in sight, but fell back several times in case he checked again. He didn't. She was about to overtake him in a ruse to ask for directions when he took a fast right, disappearing down a darkened street. When she got to the corner where he'd turned off, she realized he was nowhere in sight.

He isn't just on his way home.

Wary, Leine continued along the street, her fingers curled around the hilt of the hunting knife. The old adage "Never bring a knife to a gunfight" flitted through her mind. It wouldn't be an effective deterrent if he had a gun. Well, it was what she had to work with. Handguns were notoriously difficult to get in Scotland, although like most places, it could be done. You just had to know the right people.

Lou was good at securing weapons, but he couldn't work miracles. The next morning was as soon as she'd be able to pick one up.

Leine reached the end of the street. There was still no sign of the mystery man. She turned right and walked, constantly changing course and looking behind her by checking the reflection in windows as she made her way back to the Bomb Maker's hotel. The possible tail had changed her mind about going back to her room. Her gut told her time was running out and she needed to find her quarry, soon.

With one last scan of the street outside, she entered the hotel and walked through the ample lobby. The room boasted a polished wooden check-in desk along one wall and comfortable seating with various conversational groups punctuated by potted plants. A toasty fire snapped and crackled in the huge river rock fireplace.

Leine continued through the lobby past the elevators and down a hallway, searching for possible escape routes. An older building in a long block of old buildings, there were no side exits, but she did find an employee in a red jacket coming out of a supply closet.

"Excuse me, but is there another way into this building?" she asked. When he looked a question at her she smiled apologetically. "My husband said to meet him at the northwest entrance but I'm so turned around, I'm afraid I don't know my north from my south."

Understanding lit the young man's eyes. "There isn't a door with a northwest entrance, or a west one, for that matter. The main door is behind you, but that's south. There is a service door at the back of the property that is as close to northwest as you can get. Could that be what he's referrin' to?"

"It might be. How do I get there?"

"Follow this hallway and when you can't go any further, turn left, then right. It's a bit on the untidy side, just to warn you."

Leine thanked him and followed his directions. The heavy wooden door had an improvised security handle that was connected to an alarm but was currently propped open. Several white canvas bags filled with dirty linen were lined up along the wall. She walked out the door and onto the concrete step and peered over the wrought-iron railing to the parking lot below. Several cars were parked in a narrow alleyway in what appeared to be the hotel's private parking area. A white delivery van idled near the base of the stairs. The name of a linen service was painted on the side.

"Comin' through." A twenty-something man in jeans and a T-shirt and carrying two canvas bags slung over his shoulder brushed past her and started down the stairs.

"Excuse me, but could you tell me if this door stays open all night, or is it locked at a certain time?"

The man stowed the two bags in the back of the van before answering. "The night manager leaves it open for me, but it's usually locked." He was telling a guest what she wanted to hear for security reasons, although it was probably close to the truth.

"Thank you." She didn't ask him if the alarm on the door worked—he'd say yes whether it did or didn't. She'd formulate her plan both ways. After the delivery guy disappeared into the hotel she walked down the stairs and through the parking lot to see where the alley ended. There were two ways in or out, although the narrow lane was obviously a one-way. Leine gauged which route she'd take if she was in a hurry and then walked to the hotel entrance. Crossing the street, she stood out of sight in a darkened doorway with a view of the doors.

She couldn't shake the feeling that she was the one being hunted.

13

Leine woke early the next day and bolted down a cup of instant coffee. She'd gotten in late, but sleep eluded her for most of the night. She showered and dressed quickly and was out the door of the hotel by the time the sun rose. Grabbing an espresso at the hotel's restaurant, she followed back streets to the Bomb Maker's hotel.

The evening before, she'd noticed a small café across from the entrance, and she went there now. She chose a table at the back and ordered salmon and eggs and more coffee. While she waited, she took out her phone and checked her messages. Lou had come through with a contact that had a 9mm waiting for her if she needed it. She memorized the number and deleted the message.

She was halfway through her breakfast when Spencer Simms walked into the café. Leine groaned. *What the hell does he want?* She wouldn't have been surprised if he'd been the one following her the night before.

That begged the question why. And if he was, then why didn't he make himself known?

He made his way over to her table and slid into the chair across from her.

"What do you want?" she asked. The coffee hadn't yet worked its magic by gifting her with diplomacy.

Come to think of it, nothing usually did.

"Well, good morning to you, too, sunshine." Simms grinned as he unwound his woolen scarf and draped it over the back of his chair. A dull tan and blue plaid, the scarf was one that could be had two for twenty-five pounds all over the city. His light-weight jacket wasn't suited to the cold, windy environment, so she assumed he'd recently bought the scarf to supplement his wardrobe.

"I told you I didn't need you here."

Simms smiled and leaned back in his chair. The waitress came by, and he ordered tea and a scone. "I know, but I feel responsible for you." The waitress left, and he added, "I did save your life in Paris."

"You're never going to let me forget that, are you?"

"Some thanks would be nice."

Leine frowned. "I'm pretty sure I thanked you already." She couldn't remember if she had, honestly. Events had gone sideways at the time, and she wasn't certain if she'd actually told him. She hadn't been happy that he'd followed her that night, but it didn't change the fact that she was alive because of it. "You weren't by any chance following me last night, were you?"

Simms rolled his eyes. "What do you think?"

"I think yes."

He shook his head. "Wasn't me."

"Then who?" Her tone said she didn't believe him.

He leaned toward her, frowning. "I don't know." He rested his forearms on the table. "Apparently you do need someone watching your back."

The waitress stopped at their table and served Simms his tea and scone. Leine waited until she'd left before answering him.

"Not at all," she answered. She took a sip of coffee and set the cup back in the saucer. "What it most likely means is that our presence has been noted. By whom, I don't know." Leine's bullshit detector blared somewhere in the back of her mind. Why was Simms lying?

"Your presence, you mean. Not mine."

Leine raised an eyebrow. "How do you figure?"

He shrugged. "Salome has no idea who I am. How could she? All I did was follow her henchman from his favorite watering hole to his flat, and did it as a much older man and in a crowd. I'm not on her radar." He'd worn a disguise during his surveillance of Damil. Not one to go overboard on tradecraft, Leine rarely did much to alter her appearance other than a change of clothes and hats and glasses, maybe a wig. On the occasions she had been in full disguise, it was because the target was familiar with her, which didn't happen often.

"Unless you *were* following me last night. The only person who knows I'm here is you." She wasn't about to tell him Art and his guys were already in town. Art had texted her early that morning. She also needed to keep up the charade of cutting ties with Lou, in case Simms had been compromised.

A sad smile played on his face. "You still can't trust anyone, can you? Doesn't saving your life have any bearing on your opinion of me?"

Leine shook her head. "I'll trust you the day I'm convinced you wouldn't sell your grandmother if the price was right."

Simms gave a dramatic sigh as he slathered butter and raspberry jam on his scone and took a bite. "You've cut me to the core," he said, chewing. He swallowed and added, "And please don't bring Granny into it. She's not worth much on the open market, but she's priceless to me."

"Be serious, Spencer. You need to go home." Simms was one of those guys who talked a good game but in the end did only what was best for Spencer Simms.

"Have you seen the Bomb Maker?" he asked.

"None of your business."

Simms smirked. "You haven't." He put down his knife and scone. "Let me be your wingman. I can watch the hotel entrance while you watch the back. Or vice versa. It would be a pity to have him escape from under your lovely nose, wouldn't it?"

"As I said before, I don't need you here."

Simms studied her. "You called Art, didn't you? Or maybe that Scotsman you worked with in Paris? What was his name?" He thought for a moment, then snapped his fingers. "Jack Ferguson, right?"

"That would have been the play if I'd called in reinforcements. Why not use a Scot in Scotland?"

"Exactly. I'll try to keep from shooting any of them. But if I see someone look at you wrong, well, God help me."

"Really, Spencer. You don't need to watch my back. I'm only on a fact-finding mission here. I don't plan to abduct the guy." *Follow, yes. Abduct, no.*

"That's good, since things worked so well with Damil."

Leine ignored the sarcasm. "Besides, he probably has a contingency plan if he's found." Someone in his line of work would most likely have a no-capture policy with some way to take his own life.

"You mean like an explosive device?"

Leine shrugged. "That's one possibility."

"Ah, well, then. If you're not going to pull a Damil and torture the guy, then I guess I can back off."

That was easy. Leine studied him for a moment. Spencer Simms was difficult to get a bead on. He was good at what he did but no longer constrained by the code of ethics they'd all subscribed to when working for the agency.

Come to think of it, neither was she.

"Look at it from my angle," she said. "If I have to worry about you being made, then I won't be able to do my job effectively."

Simms scoffed. "Don't worry about me, sweetheart. I haven't been 'made' since my training days."

"Likely story, but either way, if I know you're here watching my back, I'll continually reassess the situation to take that into consideration. If you were to leave me on my own, I'd have that much more focus to achieve my objective."

"If you say so." He finished his scone and drained the tea, then grabbed his scarf off the back of the chair and stood. "Like I said before, I feel responsible. I'm here if you need me." He dug in his front pocket for some cash and tossed it on the table. Then he walked out the front door and disappeared down the cobblestone street.

Leine opened a secure messaging app in her phone and texted Art: *Change in plans.*

14

After she finished her salmon and eggs, Leine pretended to be a tourist, window shopping and having lunch outside a historic pub, all while checking hotel traffic, looking for signs of the Bomb Maker. During that time, Lou's weapons contact called with directions.

Zarko relieved her midafternoon. She went back to her hotel, ordered a rental car and paid cash. She then drove to the address Lou's contact gave her. Sandwiched between two pubs in a small village several kilometers outside the city, the tiny cartography shop smelled of ink, old paper, and fried fish. She gave the man behind the counter the prearranged signal, which he countered by saying something innocuous about the Writers' Museum on the Royal Mile. The man disappeared into the back room and reappeared a few moments later with a package wrapped in brown paper and tied with twine. Leine thanked him and slipped it into her bag before returning to her car.

Once inside, she tore the wrapping off the box and lifted the lid to find the requested 9mm Beretta with a suppressor, two Glock 17s, and several full magazines. She loaded the weapons, stored two magazines for the Beretta in the side pockets of her pants, and slid the pistol into her waistband. She put the two other guns and extra mags into a cloth grocery bag and tied it closed. Then she checked her phone and found a message from Art telling her he was in position and had some news. She started the car and drove back to the Grassmarket, where she parked on a narrow side street.

Leine found Art at a pub just down the street from the hotel. He was nursing a beer at a seat next to a window with a view of the entrance. A folded newspaper lay on the table in front of him.

She scanned the bar when she entered. There were two women and three men, and all appeared to belong to one or the other. She chose a chair to the left of Art and ordered a beer. He wore thick glasses and a goatee, as well as a knit cap with an image of the Scottish flag emblazoned across the front.

"What happened?" she asked.

"Somebody matching our guy's description left the hotel in a taxi a couple of hours ago."

Leine's heart rate sped up. "Where did he go?"

"Zarko followed him to an upscale restaurant on the Royal Mile. The guy had an early dinner and went to see a movie. A romantic comedy." The last sentence was delivered with a shake of his head.

"He what?" she asked.

"You heard me. A romantic comedy."

"Are we sure it was him? Really? He doesn't strike me as a rom-com aficionado."

"Pretty sure, although he doesn't have the full beard anymore, and he upgraded his wardrobe. Apparently he prefers expensive wool overcoats and Italian shoes." Art shrugged.

"Where is he now?"

"Back in his room. I've got Zarko covering the rear of the

hotel. You and I are on the entrance, while my other two guys are at large in the neighborhood."

"Sounds like you've got things covered." She handed him the cloth grocery bag containing the guns. He looked inside and nodded. "Why do you think he decided to show himself?"

Art shrugged again. "Why does anyone do anything?" He glanced at the bartender and other patrons and, seeing they were preoccupied with their own conversations, surreptitiously transferred the items into his coat pockets. Then he folded the grocery bag and placed it on the table. "Maybe he was going stir crazy up there in the room by himself. Maybe he's addicted to romantic comedies. Hell, I don't know."

"Or maybe he wanted us to follow him."

"What would that accomplish, other than taking one of my guys off the hotel? I had someone else cover the rear parking lot when Zarko left."

"Maybe he wanted to fuck with you. It just seems so far out of character."

"Maybe. Maybe not. How well do you know this guy?"

She had to admit he had a point. It wasn't like they ran in the same circles.

"We could sit here all night wondering what the hell he was up to," he said. "But that won't get us jack shit. Not unless he comes here to clue us in, and that scenario ain't likely." He pushed the folded newspaper toward her. "Here."

Inside she found a small radio and a wireless earpiece. She checked to make sure it was on, then slipped the radio into her front pocket and slid the earpiece onto her right ear. Innocuous looking, the equipment was similar to devices people often used with a mobile.

"What if he's being dangled?"

"It's possible. That's why I'm not out there."

"You think Salome ID'd you?" A terse nod confirmed her suspicions.

"Damil's killer could have stuck around to get surveillance photos."

Leine sighed and stared through the window at the splotches of yellow light on the slowly darkening street. "That complicates things."

"Yep." Art took a swig of his beer and set it back on the table. "Give me your phone."

Leine did as he asked and he downloaded a tracking app onto the device. He checked her signal with his to make sure it was transmitting. Satisfied, he handed the mobile back.

"What do you want to do?" he asked.

"I say we keep watching him. If he makes a move or meets with someone of interest, then I'll reassess. Grabbing the guy needs to be our last resort. If he's being watched and we take him, she may scrap her plans."

"Either way, he probably has information we could use." Art took another drink and glanced at the hotel entrance. He stiffened. "There he is."

Leine followed his gaze. The man who had just walked out the front door of the hotel matched the description of the person Zarko had followed that afternoon. His height and cadaverous appearance couldn't be camouflaged by the expensive clothes. It was definitely the Bomb Maker. Art stood and threw some cash on the table for a tip. Then he keyed his radio.

"Target has exited the building."

15

A rt and Leine walked out of the pub and strolled toward the hotel. With a laugh she turned toward him, while still keeping an eye on the Bomb Maker. A large group had arrived for check-in. Several cars were lined up outside the entrance with people milling nearby. The porter busily stacked suitcases onto a brass luggage cart and jotted information into a notebook.

"Where are you, Z?" Art said into his mic before he murmured something unintelligible in reply to Leine.

"Some asshole's just pulled into the alley the wrong way, blocking the exit," Zarko said, his tone clipped. "Backing up. Be there in a sec."

Leine nudged Art. "Looks like our boy has a meeting."

Third in line in the taxi queue and gripping a leather attaché case, the Bomb Maker's gaze flickered from one set of guests to another, never staying with anyone for long. Leine raised her head as he turned to look her way. They locked eyes briefly before Leine looked at Art to smile at something he said. She didn't think the terrorist knew what she looked like, but in case he did, she'd pinned her hair up underneath a knit cap and wore dark-rimmed glasses. That wouldn't help if Damil's killer had taken surveillance photographs of Art and the cleanup crew. Although Art wore a disguise and the clothes of a local, identification was still possible. It was in the eyes.

The Bomb Maker said something to the porter, who replied with an obsequious smile. As Leine and Art drew closer to the hotel entrance, the man's gaze swept over them both and then returned to Art. His eyes narrowed and Leine stiffened.

He dropped his attaché case, wrapped his arm around the porter's neck, and shoved a gun into the man's temple. There was a collective gasp and people on all sides backed away. Some ran for cover while others froze, unsure what to do.

"Shit." Art slid his pistol free and moved to one side as he and Leine bracketed the bomber. She pulled out the Beretta and aimed at his chest.

"Everyone, get down!" Leine yelled. People screamed and dropped to the cobblestone street. Hands shielding their heads, a young couple ducked and sprinted into the hotel.

"Don't come any closer," the Bomb Maker shouted. "Or this man will die."

Eyes squeezed shut, the porter's face twisted in a grimace of fear. He plucked at the bomber's forearm in a futile attempt to slip free, his plaintive whimper echoing against the brick buildings.

"Silence," the bomber bellowed. The porter bit his lip, beads of sweat running down the sides of his face.

Using the parked cars as cover, Art and Leine took up position and aimed at the terrorist, looking for a clean shot. A few of the guests had frozen in fear, making the logistics challenging. Normally, Leine would have no qualms taking a headshot.

But not here, not now. She wanted him alive.

"The guy you're holding has nothing to do with anything, pal." Art's voice was calm and controlled. The Bomb Maker turned to face him, forcing the porter to swivel. The barrel of the gun gleamed in the light from the lobby.

She couldn't let him hurt the porter. She'd have to take the chance that the Bomb Maker wouldn't immediately die.

Leine was about to take the shot when the bomber shoved the porter to the ground and dove into the open door of an idling Peugeot. He slammed the door closed and laid rubber as he peeled away from the curb. Art fired, shattering the back window. Leine sprinted to a nearby white Volvo, threw herself into the driver's seat, and sped after him.

"Oh, my god." The voice came from the backseat.

Leine glanced in the rearview mirror. A middle-aged woman, eyes wide in a bloodless face, sat immobile in the backseat with her mouth agape, staring at Leine.

Groaning inwardly, Leine returned her focus to driving. "Hang on," she yelled. The woman scrambled to fasten her seatbelt.

The Peugeot raced through the old section of Edinburgh, weaving erratically as the bomber blew around blind corners, tires squealing. Vehicles from all directions screeched to a halt to let him pass, horns blaring. Leine followed, never letting him get too far ahead, but remaining a safe distance behind him in case he ran out of luck and slammed into something. Thankfully, the woman in the back appeared to have been scared silent.

"I'm five minutes from you." Zarko's voice erupted in her earpiece.

"I've got a visual. He's heading toward the water."

"Copy that. I'll circle around, see if I can head him off."

"Wh-who's the man in that car?" the woman in the back asked, her voice quavering.

Leine ignored her and kept driving, the Beretta in her lap.

The Peugeot screamed around a corner, fishtailing as the

bomber tried to straighten out of a skid. Shifting into second, Leine followed. As she rounded the corner the windshield cracked, and a small hole appeared in the glass. The round missed Leine by inches. A quick glance in the mirror told her the woman had been lucky, too.

"Was—was that a bullet?" the woman asked in a high-pitched voice.

"Get down," Leine yelled as she aimed the Beretta out the window and squeezed off several shots. The woman screamed and raised her hands as if to ward off the gunfire. Her expression a mixture of shock and terror, she disappeared from view.

The Peugeot swerved but kept moving. Leine mashed the accelerator to the floor. The two cars sped up a steep side street before the bomber swung left into a semicircular drive partially surrounding a city park. Stately Georgian flats loomed on one side, a dense box hedge on the other. The bomber hooked a right and ran out of road. After a moment's hesitation, the car shot forward and through what looked to be a solid hedge. Leine raced to follow, but stopped. The hedge opened onto a set of steep stairs, leading to the park below.

As the Peugeot careened down the concrete stairway, Leine reversed and gunned the engine, tearing around the hedge to cut him off at the bottom.

She intercepted him at the foot of the stairs. The bomber cut a sharp right, and they raced side by side through the park. He squeezed off a few rounds, but his shots went wild, missing the Volvo by a mile. Leine returned fire and hit the rear side window. The terrain was too rough for a more accurate shot. Ignoring the squeaks and screams from the woman in the backseat, she hauled on the steering wheel and clipped the Peugeot's back quarter panel, sending the other car into a skid.

The bomber recovered and raced away. Leine followed, laser-focused on the vehicle in front of her. There was movement in her periphery, and she glanced in the rearview mirror. Seatbelt off, the woman in the backseat was reaching for the door handle, a look of desperation on her face.

"Put your seatbelt back on," Leine bellowed.

The woman froze, her hand motionless. "You're insane!"

"That may be, but put it back on, and I don't mean next week." Leine refocused on following the weaving Peugeot through the manicured park. Without another word, the woman promptly slid back into position and belted herself in.

"And get down," Leine barked. The woman did as she was told. Leine gripped the steering wheel in frustration. "Where are you, Z?"

"Coming in hot, nine o'clock."

Leine glanced to her left. Zarko's black SUV sprinted toward them on the roadway. They were closing in on the bomber. "Cut him off—I'll do the rest."

The Peugeot shot through an open gate and bounced onto the street, then turned abruptly to the right. Zarko came screaming in from his left and slammed into the side of the other car. The Peugeot skidded but managed to correct, heading straight toward the water.

Leine floored the Volvo and roared up behind him. Just as she was about to ram him a second time, he turned left onto a pedestrian walkway that paralleled the waterfront. She made the turn and rammed him from behind. The woman in the back screamed.

The Peugeot surged forward, weaving erratically and coming close to the edge of the walkway. A heavy chain barrier marked where the bulkhead ended and the water began. The bomber barreled on, clipping garbage bins and benches as he went. Leine avoided all but one bin, which slammed to the ground in front of her. She crashed into the metal cylinder, sending it cartwheeling into a sculpture.

He was several meters ahead of her now, but the Peugeot's headlights dropped off, telling her the walkway ended abruptly. Leine's right hand tightened on the steering wheel, leaving her left free. The other car's brake lights flared for an instant, followed by squealing tires and the sound of crushed metal and breaking glass as the car careened over the edge of the quay and into the dark water below. Leine hit the brakes and then hauled on the handbrake. Tires smoking, the Volvo skidded to a stop.

Leine exploded from the car and raced to the edge of the dock. The roof and rear end of the Peugeot glinted in the glow from a nearby streetlamp. Half of the car had disappeared. It wouldn't be long before it was completely submerged. Zarko peeled around the corner from the other direction and slid to a stop. He exited the SUV and sprinted to where Leine stood.

"Is he inside?" he asked, shucking off his shoes.

"I didn't see him get out."

He stripped off his coat and comms as the car went vertical, showing only the back section of the vehicle. The Peugeot's running lights reflected on the dark water. Without a word, Zarko raced to the edge of the dock and dove into the icy bay, striking out in a fast crawl toward the sinking car.

Leine brought her pistol up, in case the bomber tried to escape from his watery prison.

"What's happening?" Art's voice erupted in her earpiece.

"The bomber took the car off the dock into the water," she said.

"You're kidding."

"Zarko went in after him. Waiting for confirmation that he's still inside."

"Copy that."

"Any trouble with the police?" she asked. Firing a handgun in the middle of a major city in a country where guns weren't welcome was rarely a good idea.

"Nope. I disappeared right after you took off in the Volvo. With all the chaos, I managed to locate the bomber's room number. I'm on my way up to have a peek-see before hotel security evacuates the building."

"What about the briefcase?"

"Jorge grabbed it before the police showed up."

"Good job."

"Thanks. Keep me posted, all right?" he asked.

"Will do."

Zarko reached the Peugeot just as the water started to swirl around the rear bumper. He treaded in place for a moment, trying to look inside.

"Can't see anything," he yelled. He took a deep breath and dove, disappearing with no more than a ripple.

Leine waited, gaze and gun focused on the glowing taillights of the semi-submerged car.

A moment later, the car sank the rest of the way to its watery grave with a sucking gurgle. Zarko popped his head above the surface and swam back to the dock. Keeping her eye on the area of water where the car had disappeared, Leine picked up Zarko's things and tossed them to him.

"He wasn't inside." Shivering, he shook the water out of his long hair and then pulled on his socks and shoes. His down coat followed quickly. "Any sign of him?"

"No. But keep an eye out. He might be waiting for us to leave. I'll run the dock, see if he surfaces." She turned to see if the woman was still inside the car. She was. Huge eyes overshadowed a pale face as she stared at Leine from behind the windshield.

"You can leave now," Leine mouthed, indicating a nearby roadway that led back toward town.

The woman shook her head. Leine sighed and looked to Zarko for help.

Half turning toward the Volvo, he raised an eyebrow. The crumpled front end had a tenuous grip on the busted headlights, and the grill looked like an abstract expressionist had a field day with it. The woman peeked at him over the seatback.

He looked at Leine. "Seriously?"

Leine shrugged. "There wasn't time to let her out."

"What do you want me to do with him if he shows?" he asked, gesturing toward the murky water.

"Try not to kill him."

He nodded. Leine set off along the dock, scanning the darkness beyond for the telltale ripples of a man swimming to safety. If he'd been trapped in the car and drowned, that would have been a bridge she'd have to cross, but at least he'd have been accounted for. Now she had to try to catch him before he made it back to Salome.

She waited until he wouldn't be able to survive any longer in the bitterly cold water and would have to come out or die of hypothermia. "He's gotta be getting cold by now," she said into her mic.

"No sign of him here," came Zarko's reply. There was a pause. "Hey, what should I do with your hitchhiker? She's been a pain in my ass since you left."

Leine sighed. "I told her she could leave."

"I don't know, man. She's...active. She keeps saying she doesn't know how to get back to the hotel. I told her I didn't know how long you'd be, but that we could drop her off. She didn't like my answer."

"Then call her an Uber." Leine swore under her breath and continued searching the dockside. There was no sign of the bomber. The man was skin and bones. He shouldn't have been able to survive more than a few minutes in the brisk waters of the Firth. She scanned every place a man could hide, but she wasn't familiar with the area, so could have easily overlooked something. She kicked herself for not requesting night vision gear. The equipment would have made searching for the man along the docks and dark shoreline a much easier task.

Where is he?

With a frustrated sigh, she turned back toward Zarko and the woman, wondering if Art had found anything they could use in the bomber's room.

As if reading her mind, Art's voice came over her earpiece. "You're gonna want to get back here, pronto. We found something."

Leine sprinted to the car.

16

"Look at this." Art motioned for Leine to join him next to his desk. Leine, Jorge, Zarko, and Art were in Art's room at the Travelodge. Zarko had dropped Leine's now-subdued passenger at the hotel, then parked the vehicle in the back alley. Art and Jorge had come up empty when they searched the Bomb Maker's room, but then Art had discovered a flash drive in the briefcase the bomber dropped.

Leine skirted the bed and stared at the laptop screen. It was an aerial view of downtown Los Angeles. She glanced sharply at Art.

"You think LA's her next target?"

Art nodded.

Cold dread swept through her. The aerial map encompassed several high population areas in the downtown corridor. Santa had mentioned that the LAPD and FBI were worried about terrorist attacks. Too many unsecured targets. No one could be everywhere 24/7. There were bridges, historic buildings, iconic theaters, City Hall, Union Station, Little Tokyo and Chinatown, a Buddhist temple, and a cathedral, along with multiple parks and hotels. There was also the Metro Transit system.

"Yeah. Nightmare scenario." Art stared at the computer. "You'd best get this information to your guy in the LAPD. I'll let my contact in the FBI know."

Leine hadn't told him the truth about her relationship with Santa. She merely said she couldn't contact him outright in order to keep him safe from Salome. He didn't know she wouldn't contact him at all.

"Sure," she replied. "Anything else? Something that can tell us more, like which landmarks are targeted, or when the attacks are supposed to occur?"

Art shook his head. "Nope. The flash drive's clean. Just the photograph."

"That tells me someone made hard copies for planning purposes. Did you check the trash cans in the room?"

"Yeah."

She turned to Zarko. "When the bomber went to the movies, did you follow him inside to see if he was meeting anyone?"

He nodded. "He didn't make contact that I could see."

"Did he use his phone while he was in the theater?"

Zarko shook his head. "No. His actions were unusual for someone in the stages of planning an attack. I assume he wanted to see if he was being tailed."

"And you found this drive in the bomber's briefcase, which he conveniently drops when we approach him?" she asked. Art nodded. "That seems a tad suspicious, don't you think? Why would someone with the Bomb Maker's reputation leave a key piece of evidence if he didn't want it to be found?"

"Maybe because two guns were aimed at him? Tends to focus a person."

"Maybe." Leine paced the room as she thought. "The fact that the map of LA belongs to the man responsible for the explosives used in the terrorist attack on a bridge in Paris six months ago should be enough to bring in the FBI." She crossed her arms. "Convince me it's not a plant."

He turned toward her and matched her crossed arms. "If it's a trick to get you to LA, then why not mark the target? Or several targets? Why have a map of the downtown area with no identified threat?"

"To scatter resources. Think of it this way—the bomber's a known terrorist asset. Anything in his possession that points to a target-rich environment is going to be taken seriously. There are dozens of possible objectives in downtown LA, forcing the responsible agencies to cover those targets even if it means spreading their resources too thin."

"If that's the case, then we still need to find out what her plans are."

"Which means we either need to locate the bomber, or find someone else she trusts."

"Putting us back at square one."

Leine let out a frustrated sigh. "Call your contact in the FBI and give them the information. I'll go back to London and keep looking for Salome in the off chance the LA angle is a ploy to get us off her trail."

"Sounds like a plan. Are you going to need backup?"

"You guys have already gone above and beyond. This gig was only supposed to last a few months, tops," Leine replied. "Go home to your boat, Art. I hear the fish are biting in the Med this time of year."

"You sure?"

Leine nodded. "I'm sure. This is my obsession, not yours. Besides, your cover's blown." She looked pointedly at Zarko. "And probably yours and Jorge's, too. There are already too many targets to worry about. I don't need more."

THE NUMBNESS HAD FOUND ITS WAY TO HIS HIPS. THE BOMB Maker was much too cold to feel his legs cramp, but assumed that was what made his climb from the shockingly cold water so difficult.

His teeth chattered of their own accord—so loudly, in fact, that he clamped his molars together in case his pursuers were still nearby. Slowly, he eased himself up the barnacle-encrusted steps of the quay, gripping at the iron railing with clawed, frozen fingers.

The thick coat he wore was so much heavier with the weight of the salt water. The sea filled every crevice he had, including the soles of his expensive Italian shoes. He rolled onto his back on the first dry step he came to and stared at the black sky, trying to catch his breath while willing sensation into his limbs. When a tiny spark of feeling returned to his torso, he shrugged off his sodden coat and reached down to remove his fine leather shoes. They were no doubt ruined.

He'd been lucky to have gotten out of the car when he did. By the time he'd made his way to the shadowy cover of the looming concrete dock, the man from the SUV had reached the sinking Peugeot. The Bomb Maker hadn't wasted any time and struck out in an awkward breaststroke away from the scene, swimming as silently as possible so as not to attract their attention.

He'd thought he was far enough away and had started to climb from the frigid water when at the last minute he detected movement above him. It was the woman who'd chased him from the hotel. His heart pounding, the bomber slid soundlessly back to the icy depths, submerging his body so that only his nostrils remained above the surface.

He didn't know how long he'd remained that way, but his body was growing increasingly numb and he had to fight to remain focused. If he didn't get out soon, he'd succumb to hypothermia.

How he hated the cold. When he agreed to travel to Scotland, it was with the assurance that he'd be required to stay only a few days. London had been bad enough, but at least there were sun breaks throughout a few of the dreary fall days. Additionally, there was a vibrant Middle Eastern community. Because of these things he'd found his stay in Britain's most populous city pleasant enough.

Edinburgh was another story. The biting cold winds kept him confined to his hotel, and when finally there'd been a bit of watery gray sunshine, he'd bundled up and treated himself to a decent dinner, followed by his guilty pleasure: an American romantic comedy. As he was leaving the theater, he noticed the same man he'd seen near his hotel. He was certain it was him, as he had the same long dark hair and a set of striking tattoos.

He immediately called the number he'd been given and left a cryptic message on voicemail advising that he'd been followed. Minutes later, an incoming text with nothing on it but the number three signaled him to set the next part of the plan in motion.

He thought they would follow him, not confront him on the steps of his hotel. In retrospect his instinct to take the young porter as a hostage might not have been the most strategic. He panicked when he saw the man from the surveillance photos. Although he'd been wearing a disguise, he recognized the man's steady gaze.

Exhaustion from fighting the cold overwhelmed him and the bomber closed his eyes. Seconds later, he forced them open and fought to sit up.

Get moving.

Struggling to stand, the Bomb Maker climbed to his feet. He had no feeling in his extremities and stood awkwardly, his storklike legs threatening to buckle backwards, or so it seemed. With long, deep breaths, he waited for the feeling to come back to his feet and hips, enough so he could begin the long, arduous walk back.

But back to where? The thought surprised him. If he were to go back to his hotel, surely law enforcement would already be there. He would have to find another place in which to dry off and warm himself sufficiently enough to return to London. But where? It was late, he had no working phone, and he was soaked to the skin. His towering, emaciated appearance and sunken eyes tended to frighten people who didn't know him, so ringing someone's bell at this time of night wasn't an option. Perhaps the mosque he'd visited when he first arrived. There'd be no questions asked, or he'd have to silence anyone who showed an unusual interest.

The shivering had begun in earnest—he wrapped his arms around his torso in an effort to stop, but to no avail. He gazed skyward and whispered a prayer to Allah to deliver him from this unwelcome and frozen predicament. His work was important to the cause—there was no reason the Great Prophet wouldn't look kindly upon him.

But the Bomb Maker was a pragmatist as well as a devout follower, so he decided the best course of action was to start walking. He picked up his once fine Italian shoes and inverted them, watching the water drain out with a kind of detached curiosity. Then he squeezed as much of the salt water from his overcoat as he could and draped it over his shoulders. Perhaps the effort of walking would warm him enough that his feet wouldn't feel like blocks of ice.

He got his bearings and resolutely struck off into the night.

17

Heather Brody made a last-ditch attempt to catch the next wave, but her timing was off and it pulled away from her, rolling back toward shore. Surfing almost always made her hangover better, but the glowing sunrise and righteous swells weren't working their magic this morning. The shame she still felt from trying to make a move on her partner hadn't gone away with the first morning, or the fourth. Santa was being cool about it, but she could feel his judgment of her whenever there was a lull in the conversation. An awkwardness that hadn't been there before permeated their interactions. Hopefully, time would fill the void she sensed between them.

She paddled back to shore and carried her board up the beach to the outdoor showers. After rinsing off, she walked to her pickup and slid her surfboard into the truck bed, then unzipped her bag to get at her keys. She sensed someone behind her and turned. Two burly men dressed identically in sunglasses, white linen button-down shirts, and loose black pants approached.

"Can I help you gentlemen?" she asked, immediately on guard. Keeping the passenger door open, she grabbed a T-shirt and shorts from inside the truck and slid them on. Her 9mm was within reach inside the glove box.

The man on the left smiled, revealing ultra-white teeth. He raised his hands, palms up, and said, "We would like a word with you, Miss Brody." His accent pegged him as Russian.

"And you are?" she asked, still irritated at the interruption of her morning ritual, but wary, now.

"That's not important. What is important is that you listen closely to what I have to say." His pleasant smile never left his face, but Heather sensed a chill in his mood.

"Okay." She turned toward them both and crossed her arms. "Make it snappy—I'm due at work."

The one on the right stepped forward and she tensed.

"We have a message from someone who has information about you. Information that will cause you much discomfort if made available to your employer."

Heather narrowed her eyes. "I'm afraid you have the wrong person. There's nothing that will 'cause me much discomfort' with my employer."

The one on the left smiled even wider, reminding her of a feral dog.

"Ah, but there is. The event in question is a long time ago. But I doubt that you would forget the night you killed that young woman." The man's eyebrows arched above his sunglasses. "You remember, don't you? The woman who was coming home from taking her night class?" He shook his head in mock sympathy. "She didn't deserve to die that night, did she?"

"I'm sorry—what?" A chill speared the base of her skull and spiraled down her back. *There are no records. They don't exist. He's bluffing.*

Or is he?

"You heard him," said the man on the right.

How the hell did they unearth that information? Stall for time, Brody. "I don't know what you're talking about."

The man on the left sighed. "You must realize that people talk," he paused, "for all kinds of reasons."

Someone talked? Who? The only people who knew what happened that night were her father and the chief of police, and both of them were dead. Another chill crawled up her back. *The officer on duty. What the hell was his name?*

"I still don't know what you're talking about."

Both thugs just stood and stared at her, their hands clasped in front of them.

"Apparently my employer has found a witness who is prepared to testify," the man on the right replied with a shrug. "There was evidence in a safety deposit box. He was difficult to persuade, but eventually he agreed to hand it over."

Heather took a deep breath and let it go. *Roll with it, Brody. You've been through a shakedown before.* Although the stakes weren't as high then.

"What do you want?" She glanced at her phone. She was going to be late.

"My employer will contact you with instructions." The man handed her a cheap burner phone. "Keep this with you at all times. When it rings, answer it. Whatever you are asked to do, you must not hesitate. If my employer believes that you are stalling for time, or are unwilling to carry out the request, then this person will go to your commanding officer at the Los Angeles Police Department with the evidence. Are these instructions clear?"

Heather stared at the burner phone in her hand. "Very."

With a nod, the two men casually walked across the parking lot and climbed into a nondescript four-door sedan. She stared unseeing at the vacant spot long after they'd disappeared.

18

L eine threw her bag on the bed and walked to the window. The view from her room showed a slice of the neighborhood in the upscale section of West London. Manicured gardens peeked through wrought-iron gates. Maybachs and Lamborghinis and Ferraris lined the curb. Rain had been forecast for much of the day, and the weather didn't disappoint. Low gray clouds the color of iron hung suspended like cotton bunting over the city. Red taillights bled across the dampened streets below, accompanied by the swish of traffic racing by.

Spencer Simms had texted her earlier, letting her know he was back in Paris. His extended leave was at an end, and he'd been ordered back to his post as security specialist for the wealthy French businessman. Leine had drawn a small measure of relief at the news.

On the surface, his leaving gave her one less problem to worry about. If Spencer Simms was the man following her in Edinburgh, she still needed to find out why. But he presented a less imminent threat in Paris. She asked a friend from the old days who lived in the City of Light to check the bar he frequented to verify his presence there. The friend hadn't gotten back with her yet.

Not that she could relax her guard if he was there. That was never an option with the path she'd chosen.

Although she had regrets, cutting Art and his men loose gave her more maneuverability. She always seemed to work better alone, even though she missed working with them.

Which surprised her.

You knew this road would be lonely, Leine. You made your choice. Live with it.

Thoughts of Santa wheedled their way into her mind—happy times at their favorite beach in LA, romantic drives up the coast, home-cooked meals with her daughter, April—but she clamped down hard, shoving them back, compartmentalizing the emotions to eliminate distractions.

On its heels, memories of Jinn surfaced, the street kid she'd rescued in Tripoli several months before. If she thought she could make it work, she would've tried to adopt. That kid was a fighter. Leine had worked with a lot of children over the years in her role at SHEN, and she'd seen so many brave souls. But Jinn was different. Fiercer. Savvier. There was no way the world could ever bring her down.

In a small way, she reminded Leine of herself after she'd lost her parents. Like Jinn's mother, Leine's own had died after a long illness. Unlike Jinn, Leine had known and loved her father. He'd taught her how to shoot, how to think critically, and how to fight, but most importantly, how someone with integrity should live.

A few years after her mother died, her father was killed in action. Soon after his devastating death, Eric, her future boss at the agency, had found her at a shooting range in Southern California, training with whatever weapons she could talk the owners into letting her use. He'd seen something in Leine and had given her a second chance at life, at doing something with meaning.

And he'd given her April.

Too bad he turned out to be an evil bastard.

Pushing the memories aside, Leine went to the mini fridge and grabbed a beer. She popped the top and was about to take a swig when her cell phone rang. She slid it out of her pocket and glanced at the number. It didn't look familiar.

"Basso," she answered.

"Leine—it is Anatoly Sakharov. You've been trying to reach me?"

Leine set her beer on the nightstand. *Finally.* "Thanks for returning my call. Did you know the number you gave me isn't good?"

Anatoly sighed. "Yes, I realized that when my assistant gave me your messages. My apologies. The phone was misplaced in our moves back and forth from the Swan."

Anatoly Sakharov tended to conduct business on his yacht, the Black Swan, while cruising the Mediterranean. His wife and daughter often accompanied him.

"What can I do for you?" he asked.

"I'm interested in anything you might have heard about the woman whose services you used last year to remove your problem." Anatoly Sakharov had hired Salome, at the time a free-lance assassin who contracted regularly with the Russians, to take out General Tsarev, a childhood friend turned deadly enemy. Sakharov hadn't known Salome was also responsible for the release of sarin gas in a casino in Las Vegas, which Tsarev tried to pin on Sakharov himself. Leine paced the room, hoping against hope that he'd have some news.

"The last I heard, she faked her own death and tried to engineer a massive terrorist attack in Europe. I believe the attack was ultimately unsuccessful."

Leine closed her eyes, surprised at the gut punch of disappointment that washed over her. Sakharov was her last resort. If he hadn't heard anything beyond Salome's attempted terrorist attacks in Europe, then Leine had officially come to the end of the line. Correction: her last resort was downtown LA. But why would Salome attempt another attack in the US? She had to be aware of the immense risk she'd be taking if she ever set foot inside the country again. Yes, she'd had surgery, but even allowing for her altered appearance, facial recognition programs were a risk for her. Especially since she posed a threat to national security.

Still, Salome didn't get to where she was by being stupid. She'd find a way.

"Could you let me know in case you hear anything?" Leine asked. "It's imperative that I find her. Signs point to her planning another attack."

"Of course. My debt to you will never be repaid. I will do whatever I can."

"Thanks, Anatoly. I'll keep this number for the foreseeable future. Call anytime."

Leine ended the call and dropped the phone on the bed. Anatoly Sakharov was a formidable ally. He'd taken advantage of the lawlessness of the fall of the Soviet Union and made his fortune by locating and selling Soviet arms caches to whomever would pay. Later, he narrowed his customers to those who were legitimate buyers, allowing him to operate without being cast as an illegal arms dealer by the international community.

He'd made his fortune playing all sides of a conflict. He'd kept his fortune by being known for his integrity. As such, he was trusted by friend and foe alike. He also had contacts in the upper echelons of the Russian Federation and would most likely hear if Salome ended up on their payroll again.

Leine sighed and took a deep pull on her beer. She'd faced

supposed dead ends before. This wasn't the end. It couldn't be. Something had to give. She *had* to find Salome before it was too late. She walked back to the window and stared at the traffic flowing past below her.

Where was Salome?

19

"They almost captured you?" Salome stared at the Bomb Maker in disbelief. "You were supposed to get them to follow you, then lose them. That was all."

"I recognized the man in the photograph. The one at the safe house in London." The Bomb Maker's expression went from stone-faced to insolent. "As he and the woman approached I took the only avenue of escape available. What they did to Damil..." His voice trailed off. "I am lucky to be alive."

Salome swallowed her sarcastic retort. "Are we sure the ploy worked?"

The Bomb Maker shrugged. "I couldn't go back to my hotel to make sure, so I assume that yes, it worked."

She paused, her annoyance building. Was he really so incompetent? "I trust you've delivered my order?"

The bomber nodded. "Yes. Of course. They arrived yesterday at the address you specified. There is now just the matter of your last payment."

Salome cocked her head. "I'm sorry. I believe we've concluded our business." She made a show of checking the calendar on her phone. "Yes, here's an entry from a week ago with a notation. 'Last Payment.'" She turned the screen toward him.

His already dark eyes turned molten black, yet he remained deathly still. If she hadn't become accustomed to his ways she might have had a moment of anxiety. But only a moment.

His fists clenched, he said, "I'm afraid you are mistaken. There is one more payment. It is by far the largest."

Salome checked the screen again and shook her head. "I don't think so."

The bomber took a step toward her, but the two men standing guard at the door of the flat raised their Uzis and aimed them at his chest. He stood down, although the rigid set of his shoulders told her this small bump in the road could become a large obstacle.

"Surely we can work through this minor misunderstanding," he said, plastering a smile on his face.

"Misunderstanding?" she repeated. "There's no misunder-standing. You've been paid in full."

Two small pink spots appeared on the Bomb Maker's normally pallid cheeks, signifying his rising anger. Salome sighed and turned toward one of the men at the door. "Escort our guest to his next appointment. I'm afraid he's going to be late."

"My next—" The bomber glanced at Salome in surprise. "I don't have another appointment."

"I'm afraid you do." She checked her phone. "Your flight to Mexico leaves in less than two hours."

"You aren't serious. I can't go through with your plan. I've *told* you," he hissed. "I am listed on the Americans' watch list."

"Yes, yes, I remember. But still, I need you there. I assume the worst they'll do if you're captured is send you back to Saudi Arabia. Unless, of course, you are captured with materiel."

The bomber stared at her in disbelief. "But if I am sent back, I will be arrested and tried for multiple crimes. We have spoken of this."

Salome cocked her head to the side. "And that would be important because…"

"I would be put to death." The bomber's expression hardened. "Forget the last payment. I'm done with you and your schemes. My business thrives without you." He reached for his overcoat, draped over the back of the sofa.

Salome gestured toward her man who had silently taken a position behind the bomber. He thrust a hypodermic needle into the taller man's neck and depressed the plunger. The bomber reached for the needle but the drug was a fast acting one, and he crumpled to his knees.

Salome nodded at the Bomb Maker's inert form. "He'll be out for several hours. When he regains consciousness he needs to be on the plane."

The other man nodded. He gripped the bomber by his armpits and dragged him from the room. Salome watched them leave and then told the second gunman to step outside and guard the door. She returned to the dingy kitchen table and her laptop.

As she continued conducting her online research, she considered her options. It was possible the Americans might indeed catch him once he was in the United States. That would work in her favor, as well as if he remained free. He wouldn't try to escape once the private jet landed in Mexico, not with the welcoming party she'd arranged to take him across the border.

By design, she doled out only enough information to her operatives to carry out her instructions—one more reason she would continue operating in this way. None of them knew the entire plan, or where she would be next. The Bomber would not be a risk. If he was captured, then he would just be one more pawn sacrificed. She had other resources that would be less of a problem.

The game continued. The trap was set.

Pawns could be sacrificed.

20

Two days later, Lou Stokes, the director for SHEN, sent an encrypted text to Leine.

No sign of your bomber. The Brits think he went back to Paris.

Possible drowning? she replied. No bodies had been recovered from the Firth of Forth in the past few days, but his body could have been caught in the currents and swept out to sea.

Maybe. I've asked Scott to relay any pertinent information on Salome. Unofficially, of course. He was referring to Scott Henderson, the head of their old agency.

Good.

That could only work in her favor. Scott Henderson was nothing if not pragmatic. If he thought her approach to eliminating Salome would be more efficient and help avoid another attack, then he'd be the first to assist in locating the target in an unofficial capacity. "Any other ideas?"

You can always call Nigel.

No. She typed the reply before she had time to think through his suggestion.

He owes us a favor.

Leine closed her eyes and shook her head. She hadn't thought of Nigel Cripps in years. Hadn't even known he was still active. No way could she work with the guy and not want to kill him. The simpering wanker didn't deserve a second chance. Not after the way he'd treated her when she'd saved his ass and the ass of his idiot agent in Lisbon so many years ago.

That was a long time ago. You think he'll remember? she asked.

I have it in writing.

Leine groaned. She didn't have the patience to deal with Nigel "show me your tits" Cripps. The man may have an extensive network of undercover agents and be one of the most effective spy catchers in recent memory, but he was an utterly disgusting human being.

Quit groaning.

Leine typed: *???* How the hell did he know? It's not like he could hear her.

You did, didn't you? He added a laughing emoji.

Fuck off. Leine inhaled deeply and let it go. Fine. If she had to work with scum, she'd do it. Anything to be rid of Salome. She rolled her eyes as she typed.

How do I contact him?

LEINE STEELED HERSELF AS SHE CLIMBED THE STEPS TO NIGEL Cripp's four-story black-on-white brick townhouse located deep in London's posh Mayfair neighborhood. There wasn't a leaf or flower petal out of place on his doorstep or walkway, lending an antiseptic and precious air to the property. She pressed the bell on the massive black front door and was rewarded with the opening strains of Debussy's "Clair de Lune." Leine rolled her eyes.

Pompous ass.

Moments later, the door opened to reveal a man she guessed to be in his thirties dressed in a slim black suit jacket over a crisp white button-down shirt. Skinny black tie, and black stovepipe slacks completed the outfit. His wingtips were polished to a high sheen and his dark hair and pencil-thin mustache were perfectly trimmed, matching the exterior's eerie perfection. She half expected a Stepford wife to appear behind him with paper booties. The words "anal" and "retentive" bubbled to her lips, but she held herself in check. Messing with Nigel's manservant, or assistant, or whatever they called them now would not put her in anyone's good graces.

"May I say who's calling?" Mr. Perfect asked.

"You may." Leine handed him her coat and walked past him into the foyer. A massive chandelier dripping crystals hung suspended above a sweeping mahogany staircase. Muted gray walls bracketed by snow-white trim acted as a tasteful backdrop for several lesser-known eighteenth-century oils depicting the English countryside in a more genteel time. The dark wood of the banister matched the stairs, contrasting with the gleaming white marble floor.

"Leine," came a jocular voice from above. "Aren't you a sight for sore eyes?"

She followed the voice to the top of the stairway where Nigel Cripps stood, looking incredibly pleased with himself. The man's perfectly styled hair and obvious dye job screamed vanity, as did his tailor-made suitcoat, the buttons of which strained across his ample gut, threatening to pop open at any moment. If it hadn't been the twenty-first century, he'd probably be wearing a powdered wig, white stockings, and buckle shoes to complete the outfit. As it was, the bright blue silk cravat tied at his throat and John Lennon glasses gave him just the right amount of pretention.

"Nigel." Leine nodded at him as he descended the stairs.

"So good to see you. It's been *ages*." When he reached the lower level he gave her an appraising glance, his gaze lingering too long on her chest. His glistening pink tongue darted between thick lips and then disappeared. The image of an iguana flashed through her mind.

Cripps's smile morphed into a slight leer before it snapped back to its original composition. "You've aged well, haven't you?" he said, unable to hide a lascivious gleam in his eye.

Leine's skin crawled, but she covered the involuntary reaction with a smile. "It's—good to see you, too."

"Shall we retire to the library?" He turned to the doorman. "Bring tea." Nigel then offered Leine his arm, which she ignored. After a moment's awkward hesitation, he walked through a pair of double doors into what apparently was the library.

There were books, she'd give him that. The rest of the room had been decorated with more gilt and gold foil than the Palace of Versailles. The four walls were covered with gilded mirrors, lending a weird vibe to the place, as if the occupant wanted to see him or herself at all times. A deep red sofa with gold accent pillows had pride of place in the center of the room, with several expensive-looking scatter rugs strewn across the white marble floor. A gilt coffee table stood next to the sofa, with incongruously modern objects on its surface. Two gilded wingback chairs with red patterned upholstery flanked the seating area. The artwork—if you could call it that—consisted of gilt frames featuring nude photographs of large-breasted women in unnatural poses. None of the women's faces were discernible—most were obscured.

Leine's gaze settled on the only object in the room that didn't scream for a professional interior designer—or a professional of some kind, anyway—a black baby grand perched in the far corner.

"I know, I know. *Energizing*, isn't it?" Nigel sat down on the blood-red couch and patted the cushion next to him. "Sit, sit. Tea will arrive shortly."

Leine chose one of the chairs and stared at the chesty photographs. *Be good, Leine. You knew what he was like going in. Get through this meeting without pissing him off and you're golden.*

The doors to the library opened and Nigel's assistant entered the room with a tray bearing a gleaming silver tea service and a plate of bland-looking cookies. He set the tray on the table in front of them and looked a question at Nigel, who gestured for him to pour.

When his assistant was finished and had left the room, Nigel turned toward Leine and asked, "Now, what's this all about?" His gaze kept drifting to her chest.

Leine had the urge to slam the heel of her hand into his nose, sending cartilage into his brain, but she stifled it. Maiming him wouldn't be helpful.

According to sources within British intelligence, he'd been a car wreck of a field agent, always bumbling operations. But when he was reassigned to a desk job at headquarters, he'd slowly begun to make a name for himself outing double agents within the agency, resulting in a post that allowed him to command his own team within the division. Unfortunately, he was known to harass female agents to the point of several having recently lodged complaints against him.

And then there was the question of how he was able to keep an expensive flat in Mayfair on government pay. Leine assumed he wasn't playing by the rules, although it was possible he had family money or was a wizard at playing the stock market. Either way, he would have been vetted extensively when he got the job.

Whatever the reason, at this moment he was her best bet to find Salome.

"I'm sure Lou gave you the particulars," she began. His blank stare was so disingenuous she came close to rolling her eyes. Lou had told her he explained to him what she needed so that he'd be prepared. Obviously he wanted to hear it from her.

"I'm searching for the terrorist responsible for the Paris bridge bombing several months ago. We found a map on one of her most trusted people, a bomb maker she worked with in the past. The map points to an attack in downtown Los Angeles, although there isn't a specific target indicated. I believe that she's using LA as a ruse. I think she's planning something in Europe. Possibly London." She caught him up to speed on the rest and fell silent as Nigel pondered what she'd told him.

"But why would you think that she's trying to fool you into going back to the US?" he asked. "What earthly reason would she have to do so? Considering your history, I would think she'd be interested in eliminating you. You stopped her on two separate occasions. If I were her, I'd do everything in my power to kill you. Yet you say she hasn't tried."

"That's true, but you have to know her like I do. She never does anything that doesn't fit into her plans, whatever they may be. I'm convinced that killing her operative, Damil, was just the opening salvo of the game. Dangling her explosives expert at US authorities is another move that doesn't make any sense, unless you look at it through her eyes. And, she's made it a point to keep relocating. I believe she's doing everything she can to shake me or anyone else off her tail."

Nigel sipped his tea and stared at one of the larger photographs on the wall as he thought. "Perhaps. Didn't she fake her death a couple of years ago and yet come back stronger with backing from Izz Al-Din?"

Leine nodded.

Nigel selected a cookie and nibbled at the edges. "I know it's cliché," he continued, "but she's rather like a ghost. We've not been able to trace her origins, or keep tabs on her inner circle.

Now you say she's willing to give up the major players in her world. Why? What end justifies that kind of sacrifice?"

Leine remained silent, allowing him to come up to speed.

He put his teacup down. "Well, I'd have to say you're most likely correct in your assessment that she's trying to send you off on a wild goose chase."

"Can you help me track her down?"

He nodded. "Let me put out some feelers. I'll see what I can do."

Leine relaxed for the first time since she'd walked into the townhouse. "That would be helpful, Nigel. Thank you."

Nigel smiled and slid across the couch toward her. "Now that we've taken care of that bit of business, how about we take up where you and I left off so many years ago?" A glint in his eyes, he slid his hand toward her, headed for her thigh. "I have a room with several...accoutrements a woman of your talents might enjoy."

She corralled his fingers with a crushing grip, stopping his advance in its tracks.

"Stop. Now." The words exited her lips like the crack of a rifle, echoing through the gaudy room.

A look of consternation came over his face. "But I thought—"

"You thought wrong." She let go of his hand and stood. "I gave you absolutely no indication that I was even remotely interested, now or in our previous meetings."

"Well, then," he managed, massaging his fingers.

Leine studied the disappointment on his face and was ready for the petulant look that followed. Nigel Cripps could've been the poster boy for justifying the #metoo movement. "If you decide to table my request because I refused to play your asinine games, be prepared for blowback."

Nigel narrowed his eyes. "Just what do you mean by that?"

Although her first inclination was to tell him to watch his back whenever he was alone, she chose a more moderate threat. "If you refuse to follow through with your promise to help me track down Salome due to your childish fantasies, I will make it my mission to find every last woman you sexually assaulted over the years and persuade them to testify against you." She didn't bother to tell him a similar case was already in the works by his colleagues in British intelligence. So far, seventeen women had come forward and given their statements, many of whom had risen in the ranks despite his sleazy behavior and attempts to hobble their advancement.

"And who would believe a subordinate over me?" He shook his head and reached for his teacup.

"You'd be surprised, Nigel."

He waved at the air. "My reputation speaks for itself. No one would dare testify against me. And even if they did, no one would believe them."

"You're free to think what you want, but be aware there are those who don't appreciate your tactics."

"Oh, you needn't worry, Leine," he said with a huff. "This Salome character is much too interesting for me not to pursue. Should I hear anything, I'll let you know."

Leine jotted her number down and handed it to him. Then, before he could piss her off even more, she left.

21

Nigel was good to his word. Less than forty-eight hours later, he called to meet Leine with information on Salome's last known whereabouts.

"A woman was spotted in and around a rather drab flat in East London, near Whitechapel." Nigel sipped his glass of sherry. He'd chosen an exclusive club not far from his town-home for the meeting—all leather and dark wood furniture, brass accents, and forest green walls. So far, he'd been the pinnacle of propriety. Perhaps her threats had the desired effect.

"The flat's been a known meeting place for some rather nasty types for close to a year now," he continued. "The last time she was photographed was two weeks ago. She's apparently flown the coop since." He slid one of two folders across the highly polished table toward her.

The time frame matched the meeting on the bridge with the Bomb Maker. "There's nothing after that?" she asked as she opened the folder and studied the grainy photographs. One was a three-quarter shot of a woman whose body type and hairline matched Salome's, but with a cleft chin and hawk-like nose. She leaned in for a closer look. The eyes sent a chill down Leine's spine.

Salome's eyes.

"Not really—" He stopped abruptly. He'd been scanning the second folder.

"What?"

"Well, now, this might be something," he said as though to himself.

Leine held out her hand. "Mind if I take a look?"

He moved the file just out of reach and said with a disapproving tone, "Give me a moment to read the report."

She swallowed her response. She'd forgotten how childish Nigel could be when it came to sharing information. The sound of his breathing grated on Leine's already tight nerves. She drummed her fingers impatiently on the table as she waited for him to finish.

Several moments later, he cleared his throat. "It says here that the agent assigned to watch the flat followed a male suspect to a private school in West London where he took several photographs of the children playing during recess. He was then observed snapping more images of the building itself and the surrounding neighborhood."

"Surveillance photos."

"Indeed."

"Where is this school located?"

He rattled off an address in Bloomsbury. It sounded vaguely familiar.

With an increasing sense of alarm, she asked, "Is it within walking distance to the British Museum?"

"I believe it is, yes."

Leine sat back in her chair, cold dread mushrooming through her.

Jinn.

The last few messages Leine received from Jinn had extolled the wonders of the British Museum, particularly the rooms filled with Egyptian artifacts. She'd mentioned that she often went there after school, searching through the famous museum's displays until closing time. She confided that her foster mother always looked for her there first.

How did Salome find her? Lou made sure all information about Jinn was sealed. Although it had been difficult to stay away, Leine hadn't visited, much to the younger girl's dismay. She didn't want to put Jinn in danger, not while she was hunting Salome. Even though the kid lived in London with her new family, it was a huge city. Salome shouldn't have been able to find out where she'd gone.

'Shouldn't have' were the operative words.

Leine needed to end her meeting with Nigel. "Is there anything else in the report?"

"Not really. Would you like a copy? Redacted, of course."

Of course. "Yes, that would be helpful. Then I can see for myself if there's anything else pertinent."

"Here." Nigel handed her a separate manila envelope. The look on his face told her he had something further to say.

"Yes, Nigel?"

"Well," he began, clearing his throat. "Am I correct in assuming that this constitutes the sum total of our agreement? I don't have to keep looking over my shoulder, expecting you to pounce with some kind of scandalous report to my superiors, do I?"

"You don't have to worry about me, Nigel. Thank you for your help." She wanted to add, *I'd worry more about your colleagues,* but didn't. Let him be surprised.

"My duty has been dispatched, then. Well, good luck in your endeavors and all that." He rose with her and offered his hand.

Leine shook it.

"Good luck, Nigel," she said, and meant it.

As she walked out of the club, she pulled up the directions to the school on her phone.

What was Salome planning? And more importantly, what did she have planned for Jinn?

THE ACCOUNTANT WAS WAITING FOR HIM UNDER THE BRIDGE, THE tip of his cigarette glowing red in the murky twilight. Spencer Simms scanned the surrounding area to make sure that no one was nearby before he made his way to the man with the round eyeglasses and tailored suit.

"Status?" the Accountant asked. The beard and mustache seemed a bit off this time.

Simms glanced at the traffic flowing by on the street above them. "She thinks I'm back in Paris."

The Accountant dropped his lit cigarette and stubbed it out with his shoe. "She needs to be in Los Angeles."

"That will be hard to do."

"Why? Tell her you heard Salome's planning a terrorist attack in LA and provide the evidence, which I'll give you."

"I told you before she won't fall for it."

"Make sure she does. She's getting too close." The Accountant retrieved a packet of expensive French cigarettes from his pocket, shook one free, and lit it with an engraved gold lighter. He put the packet back as he exhaled in Simms's direction. Simms stifled a cough.

"Look. Leine isn't easily persuaded, believe me. She's got a mind of her own, especially when it comes to your boss."

The Accountant shrugged and took another drag off his cigarette. "That would fall in the 'not my problem' category."

Simms drew in a long breath and let it go. "Tell you what.

Give me two days. If I can't get her to LA, maybe I can help your boss figure out another way."

The other man's lips stretched into what might have been an attempt at a smile but fell just this side of a grimace. "She and the Basso woman are quite similar, it seems. When either one decides on a course of action, neither will stop until she sees it through." He flicked the ash from his cigarette. "That's where you come in. That's what we *pay* you for. Or did you forget?"

Spencer Simms glared at the man. He knew he should have taken care of things in Edinburgh. He wouldn't be in this predicament now.

"I didn't forget. Like I said, give me two days."

The Accountant shrugged like it was no big deal. "You have twenty-four hours. If she's not on a plane bound for the US by then, we'll send our own message."

"Which means what, exactly?"

"You're an intelligent man. You figure it out." With that, the Accountant tossed his cigarette into a nearby puddle and walked away.

22

L eine eased her car to the curb across from Jinn's school and parked. She kept her tinted window raised in case class let out and the kid appeared. She didn't want to make her presence known. Not yet. She scanned the street in both directions, searching for anything that looked out of place.

There was nothing.

She checked the clock on the dash: it was almost the end of the school day. Leine kept her eyes on the entrance, wondering how Jinn had been getting along. Over six months had passed since she'd gone to live with her new family. The photograph Jinn showed Leine before she left depicted a smiling, well-dressed mother and father, a sister, and a younger brother. Leine insisted that Jinn have full say in where she went and who she lived with. It was the least they could do after what the kid had been through.

The first couple of months, Jinn had sent Leine several messages through their private message board, to which Leine had replied. Mostly it was Jinn making sure Leine was still there for her while she adjusted to her new life. Eventually, the frequency of the messages had lessened as she grew more confident in her role within her new family. At the end of each message, Jinn would ask Leine when they could see each other, but Leine had always resisted a physical meeting. In addition to ensuring her safety, she didn't want to derail Jinn's assimilation into her family by reminding her about her old life.

Truth was, Leine wanted to shield her own heart from being ripped apart again. Letting Jinn live with someone else was one of the hardest things Leine had ever had to do. But the courts would never allow someone like her to adopt Jinn. Her job alone kept her on the road 300-plus days a year. To make matters worse, she'd broken off her last stable relationship.

Not great mother material.

She couldn't blame them. She hadn't been the best mother to her own daughter, April. Still, in those rare moments when she let her guard down, she'd flirted with the idea of being a role model and caretaker to another child. Probably to absolve herself of her many sins, the emotional fallout of which had been visited on April. Thank goodness her daughter had turned out to be a stable, loving, and relatively happy young woman in spite of Leine's inadequacies as a mother. They even enjoyed what had become a gratifying relationship.

In the distance a bell rang, and the front doors to the school burst open, disgorging laughing, excited children, all dressed in brightly colored coats and hats, underneath which they wore a school uniform: matching navy blue blazers, with tan slacks for the boys and tan skirts for the girls.

Leine loved kids—their innocence, their goofy sense of humor, their curiosity—and her heart broke when she came into contact with the ones who had been wronged or damaged in some way. Especially by adults who wanted to exploit the qualities she found so endearing. Which why she had decided to work for SHEN. It was the perfect fit for someone with her skill set.

As the mass of children thinned, Leine scanned the stragglers. A trio of girls wearing bright yellow hats and carrying matching backpacks emerged from the school. Leine drew a sigh of relief when she recognized Jinn by her smaller stature and impish smile. She was giggling with the other two girls as they made their way down the street together. There was something about her that drew the eye—an eagerness mixed with confidence—in the way she carried herself.

After all she'd been through, from living in a war-torn country to losing her mother at a young age and having to fend for herself on the streets of Tripoli for over two years, Jinn deserved a better life. One where she could learn and grow and become whoever she wanted.

The girls stopped near a black Town Car, and the back door opened. Leine tensed. Both of the other girls hugged Jinn goodbye, got into the car, and closed the door. Leine's shoulders inched down as she realized Jinn's friends were being picked up from school. Jinn waved as the car pulled away from the curb, and then she turned and headed off in the opposite direction.

Where's she going? Her home was the other way. Leine waited until she disappeared around the end of the block before exiting the car to follow her. She remained far enough back so that if Jinn decided to turn around she wouldn't be able to recognize her.

A few blocks later, Leine drew a relieved breath as the Greek revival façade and massive Ionic columns of the British Museum came into view. The kid disappeared into the building. Realizing she'd be there a while and would probably be picked up by her mother, Leine decided to return to her car. She turned to leave and her phone rang. She didn't recognize the number.

"Basso," she answered.

"Leine, it's Spencer."

"I don't have a lot of time to talk right now." Leine still hadn't reconciled his appearance in Edinburgh or the fact that the meet with the Bomb Maker on the London bridge went sideways.

"I just heard news of our mutual friend."

"And?"

"Beautiful downtown Los Angeles ring a bell?"

Leine froze at the mention of LA. Simms wouldn't know anything about the map Art and his guys discovered in the bomber's attaché case. Leine checked to see if anyone was standing nearby before she opened her car door and slid behind the wheel. She shut the door and locked it.

"Go on."

"There are rumblings that our friend is planning a big party somewhere downtown."

"Do we have a date?" Leine asked.

"Not clear on that, no. From what I understand, it's imminent."

"Imminent, as in I can call for an invite, or imminent, as in tonight?"

"From what I understand it's soon, but not that soon."

"Who's your source?"

He paused. "Sorry, can't tell you that. It's a bloke I met in my travels."

"How do you know he's legit?"

Simms blew out an exasperated sigh. "Since when have you questioned my sources?"

Since you followed me in Edinburgh and lied about it. "No offense, Spencer, but I don't take anyone at face value."

"Not even me." It was more an accusation than a statement.

"You know the score. Our business is filled with double-crossing, duplicitous scumbags. Remember Carlos's motto? *Fallaces sunt rerum species.*"

"'Appearances are deceptive,'" Simms said in a deeply

serious voice. "You should really learn to trust, Leine. You might like it."

"Thanks for the heads-up, Spencer. I appreciate your help. If you hear anything else, like a time or date, let me know. Until you can give me something more specific, I have to continue with the intel I already have."

"Oh? What have you found out?"

"Sorry. Can't tell you that. Gotta protect my source." Leine ended the call. Was Salome actually planning an attack in Los Angeles? If so, why? Where? Leine wasn't ready to abandon her theory that the real target was somewhere in Europe and Salome was using the Los Angeles rumors to get Leine and the authorities off the scent. Adding to her confusion, her suspicion of Spencer Simms was nearing critical levels. Was he working with the enemy? Or had he actually heard news of the French terrorist?

Ten minutes later, she cruised past Jinn's new home, a white brick Georgian located on a one-way street. Situated directly across from the home was a park, its lush lawn an inviting shade of green. Parked nearby were several cars—in particular a European-made sedan with a man at the wheel. A thin cloud of exhaust drifted from the tailpipe and dissipated in the chilly air. Leine parked a few cars back with a view of the house and the sedan and settled in to wait, her binoculars trained on the sedan.

She focused on the back of the driver's head and tried to get a glimpse of his face in the rearview mirror. His closely cropped, dark brown hair had the look of someone who'd been in the military. The sunglasses he wore seemed out of place on a cloudy day. When several minutes passed and the man didn't get out of his car, Leine texted the license number to Lou with the request that he run the plates.

Half an hour later, there was no sign of Jinn, and the man was still there. Lou pinged her back with the registration information of the nondescript sedan. The owner's name wasn't familiar, but the address was the one Nigel gave her where Salome was last seen.

Bingo. As she decided her next steps, the garage door of Jinn's house opened and a mid-sized SUV backed onto the street. The woman from Jinn's family photograph was driving. As the SUV sped off, the man in the car eased away from the curb into traffic to follow her. Leine waited a few beats before doing the same.

She checked the time: five forty-five. The museum would be closed by now. Jinn's mother was probably heading there to pick her up. Leine focused on the man in the car. He was obviously a tail. Why would he watch the mother and not Jinn? Concerned for Jinn and her new family's safety, Leine sent Lou a brief text: *Someone's watching Jinn's house. Need security ASAP.*

The SUV pulled up next to the museum's wrought-iron gate. The man in the dark sedan slowed, pulling to the side a few cars behind it. Leine followed suit. Jinn ran through the gate and around to the passenger side of the SUV, where she opened the door and climbed in. They drove off, and Leine and the other car followed.

The mother stopped at a grocery store, and then at an Indian restaurant, where she and Jinn went inside. Ten minutes later, they emerged carrying two large sacks of takeaway. True to her nature, Jinn was chatting nonstop, seemingly excited about something she'd seen at the museum.

The SUV merged into traffic, and the other car did the same. Leine hung back so the guy in the sedan wouldn't get suspicious. Just before they reached Jinn's house, Leine cut her headlights and pulled to the curb. The sedan slowed, matching the SUV's speed. The garage door automatically opened, and the SUV pulled inside. As soon as the door closed, the sedan sped past.

Leine scanned the neighborhood for additional surveillance before she turned her headlights back on and followed him.

He led her back to East London, to the car's registered address. He pulled into a designated parking space, got out of the car, and entered the building.

She parked on a side street nearby with a good view of the entrance and the third-floor window where she estimated flat 310 would be. Streetlamps blinked on as workers hurried home or to the pubs, hoping to grab a pint with friends and escape the chill in the air. One thing about being this far north in the fall, the watery gray twilight segued into early darkness, giving her natural cover. She preferred working at night. Dressed in black pants, a black shirt, and her black leather jacket, the black knit cap she pulled from her pocket would allow her to surveil the area unimpeded.

She got out of the car and walked around the building, checking for additional exits. Once she was sure she'd chosen the best spot to see whoever came to or from the property, she climbed back in the car, made herself comfortable, and settled down to wait.

It didn't take long.

Scarcely a few minutes ticked by before there was activity behind the curtain at the third-floor window—two silhouettes appeared, then moved away. A single shadow traveled past, and then the lights went out. Her interest piqued, Leine studied the entrance through her binoculars and waited.

A man and a woman walked out the front door and turned left into the parking lot. Leine focused on the man, the driver of the sedan. There was something familiar about him, but she couldn't tell, as he had a knit cap pulled low and still wore the sunglasses. Through the binoculars she could see a scar on the right side of his face. Then she focused on the woman. The cleft chin and strong nose belied a set of delicate cheekbones and narrow forehead, and she was about the right height. Leine's heartbeat sped up.

She'd found Salome. That meant Simms lied, or he had shitty intel.

She set the binoculars on the passenger seat and started the car. The two emerged from the parking lot in the sedan and turned left. Leine waited a few beats before easing from the curb to follow.

Their first stop was a local convenience store. The driver went inside while Salome waited in the car. Leine was tempted to walk up alongside the car and pop her through the window, but there were too many witnesses. And, she couldn't be sure Salome hadn't already set her plan in motion. Following her might help Leine uncover information about the new attack.

A few minutes later, the driver reappeared and hopped back in the sedan.

The second stop was a pub in North London, in an area known for its concentration of ethnic restaurants. Salome and the driver walked inside, so Leine found a place to park and again waited. Ten minutes later, they reappeared. With a casual look around, the driver slid a bulging envelope out of his waistband and got inside. Salome opened the door but stopped before climbing in. She glanced in both directions and paused, her gaze lingering on Leine's vehicle.

Keeping her eyes on her target, Leine lowered her head as though looking at her phone. She'd parked far enough away so that Salome wouldn't be able to see inside the car, but she couldn't help but feel exposed. Salome hesitated a moment before climbing into the sedan. The taillights flickered on and the vehicle rolled away from the curb.

Leine allowed several cars to pass before she pulled into traffic after them. At the next intersection, the sedan turned right. The light changed to red and Leine stopped, keeping the sedan's taillights in view. Once several cars had passed, she put on her blinker and merged into traffic.

She followed the sedan through several neighborhoods, kicking herself for not asking Art and his guys to stick around to help with surveillance. If Salome or her driver thought they were under surveillance, Leine's job would become exponentially harder and she could lose the target. Having another car involved would allow her to peel off from the original surveillance, taking suspicion off her vehicle.

You work better alone, remember? Leine shook her head at her own sarcasm. There was always a downside.

But Art and his guys had needed a break. For six months they'd all been racking their brains and tapping their contacts for crumbs on Salome's whereabouts, following leads that went nowhere. Finding the Bomb Maker had been a vindication of sorts, a celebratory event in the dry timeline of no breaks in their quest to find Salome. Then the meet had gone sideways, and Leine was certain she was staring at six months before another break.

Enter Spencer Simms, who provided intel on the Bomb Maker's whereabouts in Edinburgh. They found him and he bolted, getting away. Again, she thought she'd lost the thread and had made the decision to send Art away.

Now, compliments of Nigel Cripps, she had Salome in her sights. If she lost her, the only person to blame was herself.

Understanding that Leine wanted to fly under the radar as long as possible, Lou hadn't asked his contacts in British intelligence for help. Rumors abounded that the Russians had legacy spies within the agency. If the rumors were true, then Salome could conceivably gain access through her contacts, and Leine would lose the element of surprise. Even so, she and Lou should have tapped Nigel sooner. Neither of them liked the man, but that shouldn't have stopped them.

Working with undesirable people was the norm in this business. She'd lost count of the number of murderous dictators, warlords, wiseguys, and crooked politicians she'd had to deal with through the years to achieve her objectives. Whether she liked or disliked a person rarely entered into the equation. If the contact had the needed information, she held her nose and dealt with the person in question.

She was a block behind the sedan in heavy traffic when it took a sharp right turn and raced off. As Leine reached the end of the block, she caught a glimpse of taillights as the vehicle sped around the next corner. She hooked a hard right and accelerated, focused on the spot where she'd last seen the car. When she reached the corner, she stopped and stared down the street.

The sedan had disappeared.

23

"Take your time going back." Salome opened the passenger side door and stepped out of the sedan. "We don't want her to abort too soon."

Dmitry popped the boot and walked to the back of the car. He lifted Salome's suitcase out and deposited it on the sidewalk. Dozens of people milled around them, being dropped off for their flights. As a major hub for several airlines, and a start- and endpoint for countless travelers to Europe and beyond, Heathrow Airport was typically filled with people coming and going at all hours. A young Asian girl in a tight skirt walked by, trailing the flowery scent of jasmine. Dmitry licked his lips and tracked her progress with his gaze.

Salome yanked her roller bag out of his hand. "Stay focused," she snapped. "It's what I pay you for, isn't it?"

Dmitry's eyebrows shot up and he shrugged, trying a boyish grin on the French assassin. Her scowl made him rethink his earlier fantasies about bringing the bitch to heel.

He'd have to find another, more pliant participant.

"Is everything in place?" she asked, her tone all business.

Dmitry gave her a mock salute. "*Oui, mon capitaine.*" Something had to soften the woman. When his attempt at humor didn't work, he decided he wouldn't waste any more time trying.

"You might want to get to the airport early tomorrow, in case there are roadblocks." She checked her phone. "My flight is on time."

"And why is it that you aren't taking the private jet?"

Salome narrowed her eyes. "That is none of your concern." She abruptly turned and walked toward the terminal.

Dmitry shook his head. She was one crazy bitch, but she paid well. Better even than the general. He closed the boot and walked around to the driver's side door. Before getting in, he scanned the people on the sidewalk until he found the young girl with the jasmine perfume. She was hugging an older woman goodbye. When she turned to leave, her gaze landed on Dmitry. He smiled and checked the clock on the dash inside the car.

He had plenty of time.

SALOME FASTENED HER SEATBELT AND ACCEPTED THE complimentary glass of champagne from the flight attendant. Settling in for the long flight to Los Angeles, she raised the privacy screen between her seat and the one next to her and leaned her head back. Ten and a half hours would give her plenty of time to go over everything to make sure the plan was still sound.

It had to be perfect.

After today, Leine Basso would be on even more of a mission to destroy her. She smiled, pleased with the success of the first part of her plan. True, the Bomb Maker had almost been caught in the debacle in Edinburgh, but he'd been able to escape before the Basso woman could interrogate him. The next move would be Basso's, especially once she discovered the information Salome wanted her to find.

She ran through each scenario, working backward from her intended objective, creating and discarding possible outcomes to each. The Basso woman was an interesting opponent—many of her actions and reactions reminded Salome of her own training as an assassin for hire and informed Salome's strategy. It was as if she were playing the game against herself.

Every time Basso was on the brink of giving up, Salome would dangle another treat, reviving the former assassin's hunt for her. Salome's recovery time from the plastic surgery had been the only part of her plan fraught with pitfalls. She had to continually plant little clues to keep Basso and her security team on the right path. Once she'd recovered enough to travel without a disguise, the rest was child's play.

It was time for her next move.

Salome chuckled. Leine Basso wouldn't know what hit her.

24

Heather Brody walked into the Kickin' Boot Café and had a seat at the bar. She hadn't been inside the old restaurant in well over a decade.

Ever since her father died.

The bartender walked over and flipped a cardboard coaster down in front of Heather.

"Whatcha havin', hon?" The woman was probably in her fifties but looked as though she was knocking on the door to seventy. Brown and lined, with a cigarette-soaked voice, she had the face of someone who'd settled for a lot less than she needed to but had found it too much bother to change.

"Corona."

The bartender bent to retrieve the beer and deftly crowned it with a lime wedge.

Heather put a twenty on the bar and scanned the patrons, some watching football on the big-screen televisions that lined the wall, some checking their phones, most of them alone.

"Ever see Dougie Fredrickson in here?"

The bartender nodded, sizing Heather up. "Yeah, he still

comes in." She glanced at the clock above the cash register. "He's usually here by now. You two know each other?"

Heather took a swig of her beer. "Years ago. Been meaning to look him up."

The woman picked up a bar rag and started wiping down the counter. "The Kickin' Boot's your best bet. Dougie's a loner. Don't hang around with nobody, far as I can tell."

"Thanks. I'll give it a little more time. Maybe he'll show up."

"Maybe." With that, the other woman moved down the bar to refill a customer's drink.

Over the next hour, customers came and went, but no Dougie. Heather finished her second beer and got up to leave, when the door opened. A man walked in who could have been Dougie Fredrickson's father. With a start, Heather realized it was Dougie.

Shit, he looks so old. Hiding her surprise, she waited until he sat down at the bar and ordered a whiskey sour before she walked over. Dougie didn't look up at first.

Heather cleared her throat.

"Well, if it isn't Dougie Frederickson," she said, smiling. "Mind if I sit?"

Dougie glanced up and froze. Recovering, he muttered, "Uh, sure, Heather." He threw back a majority of the drink he'd ordered. "How you been?"

Heather slid onto the barstool next to him and said, "Oh, fine. And you?" She'd play nice—for now.

Dougie cleared his throat, bobbed his head. "Good. Good."

An awkward silence grew between them.

"You still on the force?" Heather asked.

Dougie shook his head. "No. I retired a few years back." The ice in his glass clinked against the sides as he nervously stirred his drink. "I heard you got promoted."

Heather nodded. "Yeah. I made detective."

Dougie stared at his reflection in the mirror behind the shelves of bottles, a bleak expression on his face. In a low voice he said, "Why are you here, Heather?"

Heather leaned in real close. He smelled of weed, whiskey, and hopelessness. A dangerous combination. "I'm here because a couple of Russian goons cornered me in a parking lot in LA and threatened my life. Said something about a night a long time ago."

Dougie shook his head slowly. "They threatened me, too." His words were barely above a whisper.

"What did you tell them?"

He took another sip and shifted in his seat. "Everything."

Heather groaned and looked away, her mood plummeting.

"I had to," he said low, checking to make sure no one was listening. "They already knew."

"Right. And how the hell would they know?" she hissed, her heart thudding. The bartender gave them a questioning look. Heather took a deep breath, trying to calm down. "You and I are the only surviving witnesses, and it sure as hell wasn't me that told them anything."

"They offered me a lot of money."

"You didn't answer my question. How the hell did they know?"

Dougie stared into his drink, his eyes unfocused. "I might've said something. To one of them."

"Fuck." Heather leaned back and closed her eyes.

"I was already loaded," he said, trying to explain. "I think he put something in my drink. It's the only thing I can think of. I wouldn't have said shit otherwise."

"Well, you can kiss that generous monthly stipend goodbye," Heather said in a low voice.

Dougie shook his head, angry now. "You'd never prove it.

Besides, your dad made sure your name wasn't anywhere on the agreement." He waved her threat away. "You got nothing."

"Don't be so sure about that, Dougie. I wouldn't be much of a detective if I already played my hand." It was a bluff, but he didn't know that.

"Yeah, well, you go ahead and play whatever cards you got, bitch, because I know where the body's buried." Shaking with rage, he threw back the rest of his drink and glared at her. "That girl didn't deserve to die."

"Keep your voice down," she warned, cutting a glance at the other customers at the bar. A couple looked interested.

"She was coming home from a night class, for god's sake." His voice dropped back to a whisper. "She hadn't even been drinking." He placed his hands flat on the bar. "But not Senator Brody's daughter. No, you had to prove you could handle anything. How the fuck you were able to beat the poly to become a cop is beyond me."

"I made a mistake. I admit it. But it's over and done and I can't bring her back." Tears pricked at her eyelids. God, she thought the guilt she'd carried for years was gone, but here it was, back in full force with the memory of that evening. Even so, she'd trained for weeks so she could cheat the polygraph.

But Dougie wasn't finished. "Remember all that coke and half-empty bottle of booze we found in your car? Know what I did with it and the fifty-dollar bill you used to snort it with?"

Heather's heart sank at the triumph in his eyes.

"That's right, Miss Fucking Perfect RHD Detective. I kept it all, along with the pictures."

Shit. "Can't we make a deal? I can find a way—"

"No fucking way." Dougie stood up from his stool and threw money on the bar. "You know what? I'm glad they found me. I've been carrying this shit around for too long." He spread his arms wide. Heather flinched. "I don't give a shit if they want to kill you. Karma, bitch. It'll always come back to bite you." He was on a roll, now. "And don't get any stupid ideas. I've got a failsafe built in. Something happens to me and your 'mistake' goes viral." With that, Dougie stormed out of the Kickin' Boot Café, leaving Heather at the bar and wondering if she'd be able to find a way out of the shit storm that was coming.

25

Leine cruised every block, scanning for the sedan's taillights, but Salome and her driver were nowhere to be seen. Pissed off at herself for losing the car, she drove back to the third-floor flat, hoping to catch them when they returned. She parked her rental car partway down the block and settled in to wait.

Forty minutes later, they hadn't returned. It was getting late. She got out and walked to the entrance of the apartment building. There were no lights on in the third-floor apartment, so she assumed the flat was empty. Leine scrolled through the digital listings on the callbox next to the door, chose one on the second floor, and hit "call."

There was no answer. She tried another one, this time from the first floor. An elderly woman's voice came over the speaker.

"Yes? May I help you?"

Leine turned toward the security camera and smiled. "Hi, Mrs.—" She checked the name on the list. "Mrs. McNulty? My name is Georgina Postokovich, and I'm new to the building. Second floor. I hate to bother you, but I've forgotten my key for the front door and desperately need to get into my flat."

"Of course, my dear. You're American, aren't you?"

"I am, yes."

"Oh, how delightful! I spent some time in New York when I was a girl. I was absolutely mad about Elvis Presley." There was a brief pause followed by a wistful sigh. "Tell you what—when you're finished, why don't you stop by for a spot of tea? I've just brewed some fresh."

"I'm afraid I'm late for an appointment at the moment, but I'd love to take you up on your invitation when I return."

"Marvelous, marvelous. In you go." The front door buzzed and Leine slipped inside.

She took the stairs to the third floor, located the apartment, and stopped to listen. There wasn't any discernible activity inside, so she knocked. No one answered the door. She opened her pack, found the slim set of lock picks she habitually carried, and had the door open inside of a minute.

The flat was a basic one bedroom, one bath, with a galley kitchen barely large enough to turn around in. The smell of fried bacon hung heavy in the air. A greasy pan sat on top of an equally greasy stove. The cheap Formica counter covered even cheaper particle-board cabinets. The stainless sink held a dirty plate, a fork, and a mug. There was no evidence of multiple residents, although Leine would operate as if there were. She grabbed a small flashlight from a kitchen drawer and went to explore the rest of the space.

A short hallway led from the kitchen to a small but serviceable living room, which had an older model flat-screen television secured to one wall, and a combination air conditioning and heating unit mounted on another. A loveseat, table, and three chairs filled the rest of the space. The bedroom was to the left, just off the living room.

Once she'd made sure the flat was empty, she did a thorough search of the apartment for weapon stashes. There was nothing hidden in the kitchen, bathroom, closet, or loveseat cushions. She walked into the bedroom and slid open the door to the small closet. The upper shelf was empty, but there were several shirts and men's black designer jeans hanging from wooden hangers. After checking the pockets, she glanced inside the Italian leather boots sitting on the floor and in another pair of shoes, but found nothing. The dresser next to the bed held socks and men's underwear and not much else.

If I wanted to hide weapons in this apartment, where would I do it?

Memories surfaced of the apartment she'd rented in Los Angeles before she moved in with Santa. She walked over to the bed and shoved it away from the wall with her thigh. An empty cardboard box sat on the floor. She pushed it aside with her foot. One of the floorboards underneath had a slight gap.

Good place to stash a gun.

Leine walked back into the kitchen to grab a screwdriver from one of the drawers, then returned to the bedroom. She dropped to a crouch and slid the tip of the screwdriver into the gap and wiggled the board free. Using the penlight, she directed the beam into the dark void.

Bingo.

Inside the space was a small arms cache, consisting of a tactical knife with an ankle sheath, two 9mm pistols, several boxes of ammunition, and a burner phone. There was also a well-used French passport with the driver's picture, a plane ticket to Los Angeles issued in the same name as the passport dated two days later, and a wad of cash secured with a rubber band.

She stared at the picture on the passport. Memories of an abandoned warehouse in Athens came crashing back.

Dmitry Romanov.

A powerful Russian general had hired Dmitry Romanov to kill Leine when she was working a job in Athens the year before. She'd allowed herself to be captured and taken to the warehouse where Dmitry had interrogated her. Thankfully, Art had insisted she wear a tracking device. Art and his men found them and managed to take out three of Salome's gunmen, but Dmitry disappeared in the chaos.

So, Salome had tapped her Russian connections. Good to know. Leine made a mental note to check in with Anatoly Sakharov, maybe get some additional insight. She put everything back inside the stash exactly as she found it, replaced the cardboard box, and shoved the bed back into place. Then she walked through the main room and exited the apartment.

Leine moved quietly down the stairs and through the door to the ground floor, headed for the glass front doors. She froze as a dark sedan, the same one she'd followed earlier that evening, pulled into the lot and parked in the same place. Dmitry was driving, but Salome wasn't with him. A different woman was in the passenger seat. Her head barely reached above the dashboard.

She tried the handle to a door next to her marked "Electrical." It was locked. She could retreat into the stairwell and wait for Dmitry to take the elevator to the flat, but he might decide to take the stairs and then she'd have to kill him. Which would put her back at square one in her quest to find Salome. The sound of a car door opening and closing told her she needed to move, now.

Her decision made, she turned and sprinted down the hallway, scanning the numbers on the doors. She found the one she was looking for and pressed the buzzer. A few moments later, the door opened to reveal a smiling gray-haired woman who looked somewhere north of eighty.

"May I help you, dear?" she asked.

"Mrs. McNulty?"

"Yes?"

"It's Georgina." Leine smiled. "How about that cup of tea?"

26

Twenty-five minutes later, before Mrs. McNulty went too far down memory lane, Leine made her excuses and headed for the exit, with a standing invitation to visit any time. She opened the door and quickly scanned the empty hallway. Pulling her knit cap over her hair, she zipped up her coat and left through the side door.

Maybe she was giving Salome too much credit. Maybe she really was planning something in Los Angeles and hadn't left yet. Maybe she didn't care if Leine knew. Art had already alerted his contact in the Federal Bureau of Investigation, so the LAPD and FBI would be on the same page. But like Santa had said so many times before—even if authorities knew an attack was imminent, if they weren't sure of the location how could they cover all the potential targets in downtown LA?

They couldn't.

Should she believe what amounted to compelling evidence? Or should she go with her gut and continue searching for Salome in Europe? There weren't many options. If Leine stayed in London, she might get lucky and catch some kind of lead. But if Salome was actually in LA, then Leine needed to be there, whether Salome knew she was coming or not.

Everything pointed to LA. But it still didn't feel right.

Unwilling to admit defeat, she eased away from the curb and headed for Jinn's house. She wanted to make sure someone from SHEN was watching the place. On the way, her old phone buzzed inside her bag.

Sakharov.

"Basso," she answered.

"I have some information for you about our mutual friend."

"Go ahead."

"My contact in the government has confirmed that the person in question has been engaged in certain circles in a manner that would indicate a return to that person's original role. This is on a trial basis only and involves international travel, so a rehire is not a certainty."

"Interesting." So the Kremlin had decided to give Salome another chance to earn her wings as an assassin for hire. They obviously didn't want any blowback in Russia so were trying her out on international hits first.

"As for this person's whereabouts, my contact did not have the information. I hope this helps you."

"It does. Thank you for getting back with me so quickly."

"As I said, no request is too large or small. I owe you for my family's life." He paused.

"Is there something else?"

"It could be nothing, but during the course of our conversation my contact alluded to the possibility of an informant in British intelligence."

"In what capacity?"

"I'm afraid I don't have that information."

"There have always been rumors," Leine said. "You're telling me it's more than a rumor?"

"There is that possibility."

"Thank you, Anatoly. I'll keep it in mind."

They ended the call, and Leine continued driving to Jinn's house. She'd have to let Lou know about Sakharov's concerns about British intelligence. *I'll let him tell Nigel.* She didn't want to meet with Cripps again or even hear his voice if she could possibly help it.

Leine turned down Jinn's street and cruised by someone sitting in a nondescript sedan she didn't recognize. She called Lou as she pulled to the curb on the other side of the park.

"Hi Lou."

"What's this about Jinn and her family needing security? And who's the guy that belongs to the plates?"

"I was checking out a lead from our friend Cripps, and found someone watching her house. When the mother pulled out of the garage he followed her, so I followed him. He stayed on them until they returned to the house. Then I followed him to the address you gave me, and guess who was there?"

"Salome."

"Yeah. And an acquaintance from Athens. Remember Dmitry?"

"Did you..." His words trailed off.

"Too many people," she said. "I lost them."

"You should have called for backup."

"Huh. Now why didn't I think of that?"

"Ahh. The famous Basso sarcasm."

"Sorry. You didn't deserve that. I'm just angry with myself for sending Art and his guys away."

"Didn't you have this same thing happen when you were with the agency?"

"I thought you and I agreed to never bring that up again." Back when Leine worked as an elite assassin, she'd gone after a ruthless arms dealer nicknamed the Frenchman, alone except for a Russian kid hell-bent on revenge for the death of his uncle. They'd both come close to being killed.

"Is there another instance I don't know about?"

"That's not fair and you know it."

"Sorry. I just wanted to make the point that going it alone isn't necessarily the best way to do a job. Especially one like this."

"About the job. I just got off the phone with Anatoly Sakharov. His contact confirmed Salome's back on the Kremlin's payroll. International basis."

"No surprise there. Who're they targeting now?"

"No idea. Exiled journalist, politician, former spy...your guess is as good as mine. He also said there's a possible informant in British intelligence."

"Any details, like how far up the chain of command?"

"No. But I figured we should mention it to Cripps. Just keep Sakharov's name out of it."

"You mean 'I' should mention it, don't you?"

"Pretty much, yeah."

Lou sighed. "Where are you now?"

"Back at Jinn's. There's someone watching the house. I assume he's one of ours?"

"Nondescript sedan, crew cut, early forties?"

"That's the guy."

"Name's Brock Cartwright. Former Special Air Services. He's good, Leine. Go get some rest."

"How can I sleep when Salome knows where Jinn lives? What if something happens to her or the family? I wouldn't be able to live with myself."

Lou sighed. "We'll move everyone—at least until we've swept the place. We need to make sure Salome didn't plant bugs or explosives in the house. Let me think about the best way to do it.

What's your read on Salome's timeline? Do you think Jinn and the family will be all right for now?"

"I don't know, to be honest. But Dmitry's otherwise engaged, so it'll most likely be a while, at least."

"Okay. Give me a few hours to locate an available safe house and set up the sweep. Once that's done we can reinstate the family, and keep Jinn on the move until you've taken care of Salome."

"Yeah, about that. I've got an idea."

"Okay..." The wariness in Lou's voice told her to tread carefully.

"I was thinking, why don't you and Benita foster—"

"Whoa. Hold on there, partner."

"But I haven't finished."

"I know exactly what you're going to say."

"Okay," Leine said, rolling her eyes. "Say you do know what I was going to propose. What's the problem?"

"I'm almost seventy years old, that's the problem."

"Stop exaggerating, Lou. You're not even close." If Leine remembered correctly, Lou was somewhere south of sixty-two and hadn't yet applied for Social Security, Medicare, or his government pension.

"Nita's never going to agree to that," he said. "I know exactly what she'll say—'I've already raised my children. Why the hell would I want another one?'"

"Oh, come on, Lou. That's bullshit and you know it. Nita's heart is as big as this planet. If a kid needs a home, she'll move heaven and earth to do what she can for them."

Another sigh. "If I refuse you're going to take this directly to my wife, aren't you?"

"Look, all you need to do is agree to take care of Jinn for a few months—weeks, maybe—so I can figure out what happens next." She was kicking around an idea that had potential but didn't want to commit without first thoroughly vetting the possibility.

"You know she's better off with her foster parents, right? Taking her to Los Angeles, ripping her away from her new family is going to be traumatic. After all she's been through, you really want to put her through that, too?"

"I don't *want* to. I just don't trust anyone else to keep her safe." Leine didn't expect anyone to take care of the kid as well as she could, but Lou and Nita had a stable home life—one that Leine could never replicate. The courts would have no problem granting them foster parent status. At the same time, Leine would be able to keep a close eye on her. Plus, Lou had outfitted his home with all the latest and greatest security protocols, complete with a panic room, which appealed to Leine's practical side.

"Let's just see how things play out," Lou said. "Once we're on a more solid footing, we can revisit this...scenario."

"You'll seriously consider it?"

This sigh was longer than the others combined. "I'll consider it. Jinn's a great kid. And she sure as hell loves you. Now get some sleep. You've got a long day ahead of you."

"Can you alert Cartwright that I'm here? I'd introduce myself, but it can wait." Truth be told, Leine didn't feel like being chatty. But if Brock Cartwright was worth his salt, he'd be surveilling her, and she didn't want his attention off the townhouse.

"I'll take care of it."

THE GIRL TURNED OUT TO BE SIXTEEN—A BIT ON THE YOUNG SIDE, Dmitry thought, but still worth the effort. She was certainly willing to trust him and try new things, which was odd, since she knew so little about him. He smiled to himself at the naiveté of the young.

Such easy pickings these days, especially with social media. If he ever decided to switch careers, grooming girls for prostitution would be top of the list.

He walked back over to the bed. He'd tied her legs and wrists so that she was facedown in a reverse spread eagle. Her long black hair covered the side of her face, and he brushed it back. She groaned softly. The drug he'd given her appeared to be wearing off.

Good.

His heart raced in anticipation as he gathered her hair in one hand and yanked her head back. Another groan escaped her. He leaned down so that his lips were centimeters from her ear.

"Wakey, wakey," he said in a singsong voice. "It's time to play."

The girl whimpered in protest, but that just stoked his desire. He loved it when his playthings showed deference, and fear certainly fell into that category. So much more exciting than consensual activities. His thirst for domination drove him on so many levels—he fancied himself the best of the best when it came to killing, but the really interesting aspect of his job entailed some form of painful coercion. Many times, though, his employers preferred clean and quick, rather than torture and interrogation. Which was why he appreciated General Tsarev and Salome.

They understood his need.

To make up for the uninspired assassination requests, in his off time he found candidates who would make good subjects. Normally, that meant picking up sex workers and trying out his new protocols, but every now and again he wanted to see how someone who was not in the trade reacted.

Either way, once he was finished with them, he didn't have to worry about being identified. The police would never find the body. Or, if they did, there'd be nothing to identify.

He ran his gaze over her naked backside, his erection growing. The bruises on the backs of her thighs and buttocks weren't yet yellow and were spaced far apart. Plenty of room for his particular brand of artwork. He leaned forward and smashed her face into the pillow until she thrashed her hips and shoulders back and forth, trying to breathe. Her small, lithe body was easily controlled by a man of Dmitry's size and strength.

The stupid bitch had no idea how to protect herself from predators, he thought, as he let up on the pressure. Well, he'd teach her that choices had consequences. He had to. He considered it a public service. He'd upload the post mortem pictures to *Grit*, the social media site that boasted the tagline, "Where free speech is really free." The anonymous account he'd set up led through a proxy server to some idiot in America who spouted conspiracy theories and called for ethnic cleansing. He kept waiting for a news report mentioning his arrest, but it hadn't happened yet.

He contemplated the creamy white skin on the girl's back. Perhaps tonight was the night the photographs would spark his arrest.

He'd have to make certain they did.

27

A few hours later, Leine's phone alarm went off, jolting her out of a deep sleep. She shook her head to clear it and scanned the area. It was early morning. A mist had threaded its way through the neighborhood, enveloping everything in its path. She'd slept a couple of hours, despite the uncomfortable car seat and the cold. She climbed out of her rental, walked up to the passenger side of the SHEN operator's vehicle, and tapped on the window with her ID. He unlocked the door and she got in.

A barrel-chested guy with a tight crewcut and a square jaw, Brock Cartwright was someone Leine hadn't worked with before.

"Mind if we take a little spin?" she asked.

Cartwright nodded. He started the car and pulled away from the curb.

"Anything unusual happen in the last few hours?" she asked, peering through the windshield as they drove.

"The husband caught a ride in a light blue sedan a little over two hours ago. I had Lou run the plates. The car belongs to someone who works at his law firm. He was carrying a squash racket, and was dressed like he intended to play."

"Anything else?"

"Negative. It's been quiet."

They drove in silence for a few minutes before Leine asked, "Lou tells me you're new to SHEN. What's your background?"

"Spent a few years in the SAS and retired with full honors. Knocking about at home didn't cut it, so I decided to find something to do with my time. That's when I found SHEN."

"What drew you to anti-trafficking work?"

"I got two kids of my own at home. You guys do righteous work. I'm all about saving and protecting children. It's a good place to channel my...anger issues, shall we say." He shrugged. "I'll warn you now, though. I have a tendency to go off a bit and deliver my own special kind of punishment."

"I'm going to assume Lou discouraged those tendencies?"

Cartwright circled the block, keeping his eyes forward. "Rumor has it you're no stranger to breakin' the rules," he said, his voice deadly serious. "If you've got a problem with violence, then we should part ways right here, right now."

"Not at all," Leine replied. "I'm good with whatever gets the job done." *And I'd be a hell of a hypocrite if I told you otherwise.*

Cartwright nodded as though her response put to bed any further conversation.

Leine liked that about him.

They continued to surveil the neighborhood, alert for anything suspicious, but there was only normal activity for a Saturday morning: a random jogger, a woman pushing a stroller, two kids on bicycles.

They parked in the same space across the street from the house and walked to the door.

Jinn's foster mother answered on the third knock. In her mid-thirties, Angelique Marmont was one of several accountants with a prominent law firm in central London. She wore white trainers, a pair of black skinny jeans, and an oversized white sweatshirt with the insignia from a prestigious college. Her sleek black hair framed a delicate face, emphasizing the concern in her warm brown eyes.

"I just received a call from Lou Stokes. He says we must move to another location." She spoke with a slight French accent. Worry lines etched her face as she led them inside.

"It's only a precaution," Leine assured her. "I noticed a man watching the house yesterday. He followed you when you picked up Jinn, and then left once you returned home."

"Someone followed us?" Her breath caught as the implication dawned on her face.

"Yes."

"Who is this man?" She showed them to the kitchen table where she and Leine took a seat. Brock positioned himself between the front door and the entrance to the kitchen. The smell of sausage and eggs still clung to the air, reminding Leine she hadn't eaten.

"May I ask where your husband is? He should be here."

"He plays squash every Saturday. He left over two hours ago."

"I assume he doesn't know about this yet?" Leine asked.

"No. He left before Lou called. I expect him back anytime."

Leine nodded. "To answer your question, the man who followed you is an associate of a woman wanted for the bombings in Paris last spring."

Angelique's eyes widened in shock. "Why would they care about us?"

"Lou would have contacted you earlier this morning, but he didn't have a safe house ready for you and your family, and didn't want any unusual activity to alert someone who might be watching the house. You were in no danger. I followed the man and the woman in question. They haven't returned."

"Again, why would such people care about us?"

"I believe when you agreed to foster Jinn that you were provided her background?"

"Yes, of course. We were told she was an orphan from the Libyan conflict who had been living on the streets for over two years. Was that not true?"

"It's all true. But she was also an integral part of the operation to bring the woman responsible for the bombings to justice."

Angelique crossed her arms over her chest, anger coloring her cheeks. "And why did no one tell us of this when we took her in?"

"We didn't think it would be an issue. We kept her placement with your family quiet—all identifying paperwork has been scrubbed, redacted, or sealed. Frankly, we don't know how she found Jinn. We're conducting an internal security audit to see if our server was hacked."

Angelique grew quiet as she absorbed the information. Leine glanced at the clock on the microwave above the stove. It was getting late.

"I'm sorry to do this, but we should really get going. Have you finished packing?"

Angelique shook her head. "No. I wanted to hear the entire story before I committed to moving. How long do you think we will need to be away?"

"It should only be for a day or two. Once our team is finished clearing your home, you'll be good to go."

"It would have been better if your organization had let us know about these people who are looking for Jinn," Angelique said, obviously annoyed. "At least my husband and I would have been prepared for such an eventuality. We have many things planned this weekend that are difficult to cancel."

"You're right. I'm sorry." Leine caught her gaze and held it. "But continuing to stay in this house may put you, your husband, and your children in danger. For your safety, you need to take this step. I know it will be disruptive—"

"Disruptive? You think sweeping our home for bombs and surveillance equipment will be *disruptive*?" Angelique said, incredulous. "Why would uprooting three children and their parents in the middle of a Saturday morning, removing them from their home, their friends, their routines, be disruptive?" She scoffed and turned away, shaking her head. "This is absolutely ridiculous. We can't do this."

"Angelique. Look at me." Leine waited until the other woman looked at her. "I know this is a terrible thing to have to do with no warning. I know how hard this is for you and your children." She took Angelique's hands in hers. They were cold to the touch, as though the blood had seeped out. "But if you stay, you could lose one or all of them, as well as your home. Their lives are worth so much more than that."

Angelique didn't say anything but continued to hold Leine's gaze. A few moments later, her shoulders sagged.

"Poor, sweet Jinn," she said, closing her eyes. When she opened them, resolve had replaced confusion and fear. "I must finish packing." She rose from the table.

"Do you need help?" Leine asked.

"No, thank you."

"May I speak with Jinn?" Leine glanced beyond the kitchen to the living room.

"She's not here."

Leine froze. "Where is she?" She glanced at Cartwright, who narrowed his eyes.

"She went to the museum like she always does," Angelique said. "I didn't know there was a problem."

"I didn't see her leave," Cartwright said.

"She usually goes out the back door. There's a shortcut through the alley." Angelique glanced at him, then at Leine. "She left before I received the call from Lou."

"When is she supposed to be back?"

"I texted her as soon as I finished speaking to Lou, telling her to come home at once. Let me check—" She pulled her phone from her back pocket and looked at the screen. "She hasn't responded yet."

"Is that unusual?" Leine asked.

Angelique shook her head. "Sometimes she ignores me if she's found something particularly interesting." She typed another text and hit the send button. "I just told her it was very important and that she needs to come home now." She was about to lay the phone on the table when she frowned and tapped the screen. The blood drained from her face.

"What is it?" Leine asked.

Angelique brought her hand to her mouth. "There's been an explosion." She locked eyes with Leine and turned the screen toward her. "At the British Museum."

28

Angelique's husband arrived just as Leine was leaving for the museum. Cartwright would remain at the house to help facilitate the family's move. Salome may have planned a second phase, and Leine wanted everyone out and safe as soon as possible. He assured her he'd get them on the road to the safe house within twenty minutes.

Leine made it to the British Museum in record time. She got as close to the museum as she could before first responders ordered her to stay back. She pulled to the curb and got out of the car. Chaos and disbelief clung to the air.

The Ionic columns at the entrance were still in one piece, although rubble filled the landing. Pandemonium ruled the courtyard. Dozens of people milled about, panicked, some screaming for their loved ones, many sobbing in distress, others with blank faces, obviously in shock. A woman held a blood-stained sweatshirt to her head, blood streaming down her face. Two older Asian women clasped each other's shoulders, crying. A toddler screamed in his father's arms. First responders with gurneys threaded their way through the crowd as police officers worked to clear a path.

Heart in her throat, Leine pushed through the throng, scanning the courtyard for Jinn. Casualties spilled from the museum with blood on their clothes. When she reached the entrance gate, a black-coated police officer barred her way.

"No one is allowed in," she said.

"But my child is in there," Leine said. She didn't have to act concerned. She was.

Compassion flickered across the woman's face. "There's a place set up for relatives and friends over there." She nodded toward a small group of people in an area cordoned off with yellow crime scene tape.

"How many casualties?" Leine asked.

"I'm sorry, but I can't give you that information right now. Why don't you go over there and join the others? We'll be sure to let you know as soon as we can."

"What happened?" Leine asked. It could have been a gas leak, although initial news reports had dismissed the idea, citing a possible terrorist attack.

"We don't know yet."

"It wasn't a gas leak, was it?"

The police officer looked away. "It doesn't appear to be, no."

Leine thanked her and moved into the courtyard. There was still no sign of Jinn. The more she saw, the more convinced she was that this was the work of Salome. The similarities to a bombing at Notre Dame the spring before were chilling.

She walked toward the group of people awaiting word of loved ones. There was no officer in sight, so she kept going, slipping past the crowd and into the main courtyard. Dressed in black and acting as though she belonged, no one paid attention to her as she followed two paramedics transporting a gurney up the steps and through the entrance.

Scattered among the shards of glass and rubble from the explosion were the obvious remains of a suicide bomber, cementing in Leine's mind that this attack had Salome's signature. Blood and bones and bits of flesh and brains streaked the highly polished marble floor of the Great Court. Leine picked her way through what appeared to be randomly scattered ball bearings and nails. Nothing about this attack had been random. C-4, the explosive material ordinarily used in suicide vests, would have been packed with as many projectiles as the impressionable material could hold, for more damage, more impact.

More casualties.

The wounded were being tended, and the dead that hadn't yet been removed—she stopped counting at twelve—were being placed in body bags and wheeled out through the main door. Relief flowed through her when she got to the last body and realized that none of them were Jinn.

Leine circled the massive Great Court, pushing past shell-shocked employees and the various shops and bookstores and cafés, before she returned to the place she'd started. It wasn't until then that someone thought to stop her.

"Where's your identification?" The police officer didn't look happy.

"I'm looking for my daughter," Leine said, adding a slight quaver to her voice. No point in trying to bluff her way out of it.

"I'm afraid you aren't authorized to be here. There's a place for you to wait outside in the courtyard." He took her gently by the arm and led her to the entrance. "It's just over there, see?"

"I do. Could you please tell me if an eleven-year-old girl was —" She paused for a moment. "If anyone found an eleven-year-old girl? One who's small for her age and goes by the name of Jinn?"

The officer shook his head. "I'm afraid I have no idea. If you would please go over to the group, I'm sure someone will be with you in due time."

Leine thanked him and headed back toward the people

waiting for news. *What if Salome abducted Jinn? What if Jinn was one of the first casualties and they've taken her away already?* Leine would check with local hospitals first, then the morgue. A shiver ran along her spine at the thought of identifying the kid in a cold, antiseptic morgue.

"Wait for me!"

Leine froze. That voice. She turned to see who had yelled, but only saw a young girl running to catch up with an older woman. Leine was about to turn back when she caught a glimpse of a face. A small, heart-shaped, elfin face.

She started to walk toward her. The crowd parted, revealing the eleven-year-old—all four foot six of her. A pixie haircut framed almond-shaped, dark brown eyes, tilted at the corners, and topped by slightly pointed ears giving her a fairy-like appearance, and two of the reasons for her nickname, Jinn of the Marketplace. Leine's heart squeezed tight as the young girl let out a painful sob and barreled straight for her. She threw her arms around Leine's waist and buried her face in the folds of her jacket. Leine pulled her in for a bear hug.

"You're here," was all Jinn could manage between sobs.

"I'm here, Jinn," Leine murmured as she stroked her hair. "I'll always be here."

29

Leine walked Jinn and her chaperone to Gatwick Airport security and handed the kid her backpack.

"When will you come to Los Angeles?" Jinn asked for the sixth or seventh time.

Leine smiled and knelt down so she was at eye level. She straightened Jinn's collar and smoothed her jacket. "I told you, when my business is finished over here." She eyed the gloves sticking out from her jacket pocket. "You know you're probably not going to need those when you get to LA, right?"

Jinn nodded, her dimples deepening as she smiled. "I know. I want to have them, just in case. You're sure Angelique and David and Serena and Robert will be all right?"

Leine looked her in the eye and said, "I promise they'll be safe. There will be people watching the house when they come back, just in case. Please don't worry, sweetie."

A kid this young shouldn't have to worry about their family or friends being the target of a terrorist attack. After her and Jinn's tearful reunion at the museum, Leine had asked Lou to book a flight for Jinn and a chaperone to Los Angeles that afternoon. The desire to find Salome and wipe her off the face of the earth burned deep, and she wanted to make sure Jinn was as far away as possible.

Within an hour of the museum bombing, Jinn's foster family had been tucked away in one of SHEN's safe houses outside of London. The bomb and bug detection crew were already at work on the townhouse, combing every inch of the structure and grounds. With any luck, the family would be back in the house, sans Jinn, in twenty-four hours or less.

Jinn wrapped her arms around Leine's neck and kissed her on both cheeks. Leine returned the embrace but was the first to break contact. Tears brimmed in Jinn's eyes, which she wiped away. Although she'd made friends at the private school and she liked her new arrangements, when she was told she was being moved to Los Angeles for her own safety and the safety of her foster family, she embraced the idea enthusiastically. Lou called his wife, Benita, who immediately agreed to have Jinn stay with them.

Leine had another idea but decided not to share it with her yet. She still had to take care of the Salome problem. Once that was achieved, she'd be able to give the idea more thought.

Jinn's chaperone, a middle-aged woman named Jessica, pointed to her watch. Leine nodded.

"Looks like it's time to go." She gave Jinn another quick hug and then stood. "Have fun, okay? I'll be there before you know it." She ruffled the kid's hair and smiled at Jessica. "You take care of her, all right? This girl's very special."

Jessica smiled at Jinn. "You know I will. We'll both be seeing California for the first time. It's very exciting."

"Jessica says she's going to take me on a tour of movie star homes." Jinn rolled her eyes.

Jessica laughed. "Don't be cheeky. It's going to be great fun."

Jinn rolled her eyes again, but Leine could tell she was looking forward to the trip. The two walked over to stand in line.

Jessica helped Jinn put her backpack on the metal table, and they removed their shoes. Jinn looked over at Leine and smiled. It was the smile of a kid who was hoping for the best but had the best pulled out from under her so many times she couldn't trust it.

Leine was going to make sure that didn't ever happen to her again.

"Safe travels," Leine called as they walked through security. She watched until the two of them disappeared from view.

Leine had just merged into traffic leaving the airport when Lou called.

"The Bomb Maker's been spotted in San Diego," Lou said.

"He what?" Leine replied, surprised. *So he didn't drown that night in Edinburgh.* His presence in Southern California added to the overwhelming evidence that Salome was planning something in LA. But why allow himself to be seen so easily? He could have gone to ground until it was time to put Salome's plan into motion.

"This doesn't feel right. Was he incognito?" Surely he'd attempted to conceal his identity.

"No. DHS ID'd him as Faizah Hajjar from Tabuk, address somewhere near Paris. There's no record of entering the US. He's on a French counterterrorism watch list. He's suspected of building vests for the attacks last spring, but there's no hard evidence."

So Faizah Hajjar, aka the Bomb Maker, had been on French CT radar for months. As far as Leine knew, they hadn't shared the information with any American intelligence agencies, unless Paul Miller hadn't told Leine everything.

"Why would Salome risk sending him to the States? She must have known he was on a watch list."

"Decoy?"

"But why sacrifice another operative?" Especially someone who had sought-after skills like bomb making. To what end? Leine stared out the windshield as the rain and wind buffeted the car.

"Don't know what to tell you. But it's something we need to pay attention to."

"What are they going to do with him?"

"The FBI have him under surveillance, but that's as far as they'll go right now. The Saudis lodged an extradition request. They have a list of grievances against him. Scott stepped in to make sure he doesn't go anywhere yet." He was referring to Scott Henderson, the head of the agency Lou and Leine both worked for in a previous life.

"Maybe I'm wrong."

"You weren't wrong, Leine. The British Museum wasn't an afterthought. That took planning. But everything points to LA now. What do you want to do?"

Leine thought for a moment. The idea still didn't sit well with her. Her instincts told her to proceed carefully.

"There's no way she'd make such obvious moves unless she was playing me."

"Could be she's underestimating you."

"Possibly. But I doubt it." Salome hadn't risen to her position in Izz Al-Din, a fierce, male-centric terrorist organization based in North Africa by underestimating her enemies. She was currently persona non grata in the terrorism community after her failed attempt to bring the West to its knees the previous spring. Her agreeing to a trial period with the Russians was undoubtedly her way of engineering a comeback.

Getting the band back together, terrorist style.

"Hold on a second." She pulled to the curb and brought up the British Airways website on her phone. There were several seats available on the same flight as the one Dmitry would be on the next day. Leine booked a seat several rows back from his. She'd have to be careful and wear a disguise since Dmitry knew her by sight, but it had been a while and seeing her would be out of context, so she didn't think he'd recognize her. Following him would give Leine a chance to find out where Salome was holed up.

"I'll be on British Airways flight number 0283 to LAX tomorrow, arriving 13:05. The same as Dmitry. I'll send details."

"I'll send backup."

"Copy that."

This time she'd make sure she didn't lose the target.

30

Bounds ritish Airways flight number 0283 arrived at the gate three minutes early. Leine stood in the aisle, looking down at her phone, waiting to deplane. Dmitry Romanov had been chatting up a pretty little brunette in the seat next to him and hadn't noticed Leine sitting several rows back. If he turned around now, he wouldn't recognize her anyway.

She wore a blond wig tied in a messy bun and oversized designer sunglasses. Those two changes used in combination with a brimmed hat, dark pink lipstick, and a designer outfit were so far out of character she doubted even Lou would recognize her.

She kept an eye out for anyone who looked like they were waiting for Dmitry as she followed him through customs and immigration, and relaxed a bit once she spotted one of Lou's people in the main terminal. The nondescript man in his mid-thirties with sandy hair and a phone in his hand went by the name of Jim Recker. Leine shifted her bag to her left hand, indicating the target was in front of her and to her left. Recker acknowledged by tapping his leg once.

Looking at his phone, Recker walked straight into Dmitry, knocking him off his stride. Dmitry's carry-on bag slid off his shoulder and dropped to the floor. Recker immediately picked up the bag and handed it back to him, obviously apologizing for his clumsiness. With a frown of annoyance, Dmitry said something and Recker nodded, apparently relieved. As Dmitry walked away, Recker scratched the side of his nose, indicating that he'd successfully placed the tracking device.

Leine continued to follow Dmitry through the main terminal to baggage claim. Recker paralleled them and exited through a pair of glass doors to their left. When Dmitry reached a different set of doors, she hung back near the baggage conveyor as though waiting for her luggage and scanned the area for Salome's thugs. Dmitry pulled out his phone, typed something, and then walked outside. Leine sent a text to Lou giving their location near baggage claim before going through another set of doors to follow Dmitry outside.

It was a typical, sunny Southern California day. A light breeze ruffled the brim of her hat, bringing with it the scent of exhaust and cigarette smoke. She let her carry-on bag slide to the sidewalk, took her phone out of her pocket, and pretended to check her messages.

Several minutes later, a midnight blue, late-model Navigator with dark windows pulled to the curb in front of Dmitry. He opened the front passenger door and climbed in. Leine texted the plate number to Lou as a white four-door sedan pulled to the curb alongside her. The passenger window rolled down, revealing a woman about Leine's age with curly black hair in the driver's seat.

She smiled at Leine and said, "Lou sent me to pick you up. He said to tell you it's raining in Seattle."

"Yes, but the coffee's good," Leine answered, using the second part of the prearranged code to identify herself. She opened the back door and tossed her bag inside, then climbed in the passenger seat. "Follow the dark blue SUV," she added, nodding toward the Navigator. It was now half a block away, barely crawling through traffic.

"I'm Kathy McNabb," the woman said as she merged with the other cars. They were several vehicles behind the Navigator.

"Leine Basso." Leine accessed the tracking and audio monitoring app on the cloud and paired it with the device Recker had planted on Dmitry's carry-on. Lou had conveniently labeled it SHEN3. The battery operated tracker had audio capabilities but would only transmit a few hours, at best, and not very far. The geolocator used very little juice and would outlive the audio portion by several days, as long as Dmitry didn't stumble onto it. She inserted an earbud and clicked on the audio portion of the application.

"Good to see you, my friend," a man with a deep Russian accent said. Music played quietly in the background.

"Let's be clear. I'm not now, nor will I ever be, your friend." Leine recognized Dmitry's voice. "What's the plan?"

There was a slight pause before the other man answered. "I am to deliver you to a safe house. You will await further instructions there."

The answer was followed by an impatient sigh. "When's the meeting?"

"Relax. Everything is according to plan. You will meet when the time is right."

"Fine."

"Please open your shirt," the Russian said.

Another sigh. "Does she really think I would betray her?"

"Open your shirt."

The sound of rustling fabric came through the mic. "See? Nothing. No radio, no wires, nothing. If you'd like, I can remove my pants so that you can look at my gigantic balls."

The Russian paused. "That won't be necessary."

Leine drummed her fingers on the armrest waiting for more conversation, but there was only road noise and the radio.

Kathy did her job well. Her actions appeared random, but she always managed to make the lane changes needed to keep the Navigator close enough for monitoring the audio. Recker, now wearing a baseball cap, a pair of sunglasses, and a different shirt, caught up to them driving an older-model Chevy. They communicated briefly through wireless earpieces.

"You guys work well together," Leine commented, glancing in the side mirror at the vehicles behind them. "Is there a third vehicle?"

Kathy nodded toward the rearview mirror. "Miguel and Vernon are on the other side of the Navigator in that white Toyota pickup."

Kathy glanced at Leine. "You and Stokes have known each other a long time, right?"

Leine nodded. "Since I was a teenager. You can always count on Lou to have your back. He's a master of logistics."

"He certainly knows his stuff."

Leine had worked with most of the operatives before but hadn't met Kathy or Vernon. People came and went at SHEN. The burnout rate was high. Witnessing the stark consequences of human trafficking day-in and day-out was tough to take. Leine had learned to compartmentalize her emotions early in her life as an assassin and tended to be less affected than the others. Still, her kill wall told her the job was getting to her, too.

Which was why she'd transitioned to hunting Salome after the Paris bombing. Yet here she was, back working with SHEN and putting these people's lives in danger.

The Navigator exited the freeway and headed north. Kathy and Leine continued on the freeway past the off-ramp. They would circle back using a different route. The white Toyota carrying Miguel and Vernon exited with the Navigator, with Recker following.

A few blocks later, the green dot that represented the SUV turned right. Kathy relayed to Leine that Miguel and Vernon would continue going straight, letting Recker take the lead. Miguel would hang right at the next corner and parallel them. There was still no conversation between Dmitry and the Russian.

The neighborhood they were in was somewhere south of middle class, but the postage-stamp-sized yards and older sidewalks were clean and tidy. There was no sign of gang activity, which was surprising in that part of the city.

The SUV continued for a few more blocks where the properties began to look less inviting, and spray painted gang signs were the artwork *du jour*. Kathy and Leine circled back and caught up to the others, turning onto the street several cars behind the Navigator.

"Wait a minute." Dmitry's voice had an edge. "There's a car back there. I've seen it before. At the airport."

"What do you want me to do?" the Russian asked.

"Turn left at the light. I want to see if they follow."

Kathy updated the team and turned right at the next intersection.

The blinking green dot on the tracking app took a left turn.

A moment later, the Russian's voice came through Leine's earbuds. "It was nothing."

Dmitry replied, "Drive past the house one block, then circle back."

A few minutes ticked by before Dmitry spoke again. "If someone was following us, we lost them."

"Do you think we've been compromised?" asked the Russian.

"I don't think so."

Leine and Kathy watched the green dot turn right and then

right again as the SUV circled the block. After a few minutes, the dot stayed in one place, indicating the vehicle was stationary. Leine tapped the dot, bringing up the address.

Leine gave it to Kathy, who relayed the information to the team.

"Got it," said Recker "I'm on first watch. Vernon and Miguel will take the second shift. Kathy's down for the one after that. Do you have a preference, Leine?"

"No. Just let me know when you want me here." Leine turned to Kathy. "How long are your shifts?" Depending on the objective, watches could be anywhere from four to eight to twelve hours. It was a far cry from having to do it on her own. It was also one of her least favorite jobs, and she'd been doing it a lot lately.

"If you're alone, it's a four-hour shift. Eight hours with two."

"So I have at least sixteen hours before you need me, right?"

Kathy nodded. "Probably longer. Give it twenty-four. Unless you have something you need to do, then we can cycle again if you need the time. Just let us know."

"Thanks. That gives me some leeway." Leine texted the link to the listening app to the rest of the team so they could hear what was going on while she was gone. She didn't expect Salome to be there. If she had, it would have been even more suspicious. "Do you guys have a mic?" A parabolic mic would give them access to conversations happening inside the house once the tracker's audio capabilities crapped out.

"Yeah. Miguel and Vernon have one in the pickup."

"Perfect. Keep me posted."

"Will do," Kathy said. "Where would you like to go?"

Leine hesitated, the reality of her situation sinking in for the first time since she'd left LA. She hadn't been back in the States for over six months. Even then, she'd only stayed long enough to ensure April's safety and to publicly break things off with SHEN and Santa. Before that, she'd been on the road in Libya for close to a year.

Not exactly conducive to keeping a long-term relationship alive. Sadness welled up inside of her at the thought of the severed relationship with Santa. She closed her eyes and locked the pain in an imaginary box inside her mind. She'd deal with it later, when she was finished with Salome.

The reality was she didn't have a home. *You've been here before, Leine.* It was time to go back to how she lived prior to moving in with Santa. He'd moved her stuff over to April's a few months before. Her daughter had an extra couch, but Leine couldn't be seen anywhere near her. Yes, she had round the clock security, but that wouldn't stop Salome if she knew where April was living.

She checked the time. It was close to five. Lou would still be at his desk. He usually worked until six or seven, depending on the caseload. But she couldn't be seen going to SHEN headquarters. Not if Salome was in Los Angeles. She wouldn't take the chance of putting him or any of the operatives in danger. They'd have to meet somewhere Salome wouldn't expect.

"Take me to a hotel."

31

Heather Brody stared at the cell phone in her hand. She couldn't do it. It went against everything she'd done with her life. Everything except that fatal night so many years before when she'd made such a huge mistake.

And now it had come back to haunt her.

The woman on the phone assured her that no one would get hurt. Part of her wanted to believe the caller's words, but the other, more cynical part of her, forged from years of working criminal cases, told her it was a lie.

What choice did she have? If she didn't do as the caller asked, her entire life would come crashing down in a fiery conflagration of bitter recrimination and prison time. All the years of hard work, of busting her ass to be the best, to close the most cases, to prove beyond a shadow of a doubt that she could match and exceed the best minds in the department—all of that would be gone in an instant, all because her past had caught up with her.

She couldn't see a way out. If she went to her commanding officer and told him what was happening, he'd immediately suspend her until an investigation could prove one way or another whether she was fit to serve.

That investigation would prove she was not. It would prove that she was a liar, a cheat, and a murderer.

Scratch that. There was no intent. It wasn't cold-blooded murder.

Hadn't she straightened up afterward and turned her life around? She had to, upon pain of being disowned by her straight-as-an-arrow father, something she couldn't endure. She'd always been his favorite child, even when she began to show signs of rebelliousness in her teens. He'd explained it away by saying she was "spirited" and "unconventional." That night long ago wasn't spirited or unconventional behavior. It was a flat-out disregard for the law, for human life, for the physical limits of an eighteen-year-old college student with a bright, shiny future, a fast car, and a lot of drugs and alcohol.

How many drinks had she had that night? Eight? Ten? She couldn't remember. It had been a party at some boy's parents' home. She'd done cocaine—everyone in that crowd did, and if you didn't, you had to go play with the normal people. Not the rich, popular, out of control assholes she'd called friends.

And, of course she'd smoked a shitload of weed. She loved weed back then.

After leaving the party, she blacked out at the wheel of her vintage Ford Mustang, wrecked the finest car she'd ever owned. She could've wrapped it around a tree like a classmate did earlier that year. But no, she had to plow into the rear end of a Volkswagen Beetle, killing the driver, a woman a few years older than Heather, who had just finished her last night class and was going home to celebrate.

The guilt Heather carried from that night had spurred her on, made her prove to herself and everyone around her over and over that she was worthy of her father's love and the respect of her peers.

But she wasn't worthy. She was shit. And she was going to prove it again by what she was about to do.

She tapped in the number and brought the phone to her ear.

32

L eine had just checked in to her room at the hotel and was about to verify the ETA of her rental car when her cell phone buzzed. She glanced at the screen. It was Lou.

"Hey, Lou."

"Hey. Which room are you in?"

She told him and hung up. Five minutes later, there was a knock on the door. Leine let him in, then closed and locked the door. Lou heaved the black duffel bag he was carrying onto the bed. He glanced out the window at the stellar view of the parking lot.

"Nice," he said, taking a seat at the table next to the window.

Leine unzipped the bag and did a quick inventory. Everything she'd requested was there: one 9mm Beretta with a suppressor and extra magazines, one Heckler & Koch MP5SD submachine gun with a suppressor and three 30-round mags, two flash bang grenades, a lightweight bullet proof vest, a pair of night vision goggles, or NVGs, and a sniper rifle with a scope and cartridges.

Lou gave her a sideways glance. "Starting a war?"

"A girl can never have too many tools." She zipped the bag closed and joined him at the table. "Art alerted the FBI and the LAPD about the map he found in the Bomb Maker's case," she said. "They're conducting surveillance of several particularly vulnerable targets for the time being, like the transit system and a couple of landmarks, although I've been told neither organization will be able to continue indefinitely."

"Looks like they're doing the best they can with the intel they have."

"I don't think downtown is the actual target."

Lou gave her a sharp look.

"Finding this map was too easy," she explained. "I think it's a bid by Salome to throw police off the track. Make it so resources are stretched thin."

Lou nodded, acknowledging her point. "But what if you're wrong? They've got to go on what they have, not on some gut feeling."

"How many times have I been wrong in twenty years? Twice? Three times, maybe?"

"Then give me your assessment," Lou said. "Tell me where you think she's planning to hit."

"I don't know yet."

"You still believe this is an elaborate ruse to put you and the authorities off the scent." It was a statement, not a question.

"Yes, I do." Leine leaned forward in her chair. "I'm not discounting the idea that she's planning an attack here in LA. In fact, I think there's a high probability that she is. The thing is, we don't really know."

"The British Museum bombing killed twenty-seven people. I'd say that qualifies as big."

"That was the equivalent of a test run." Leine sat back and crossed her arms. "You know how she operates. She's not one to think small."

Lou sighed and stared out the window. Noises from rush hour traffic on the street below filtered through the pane. "When's your meeting with the FBI?"

"Tomorrow afternoon."

"And you're going to tell them your theory?"

"Of course. I'm going to try to convince them to think like she does."

"You're in favor of reducing the resources they're currently using?" he asked.

She nodded.

"And which targets are you going to suggest they concentrate on?"

"Like I said, I don't know yet."

"That won't fly."

"I know. I need more information." She checked the time on her phone. "I'm due to check in with Recker, see if he's gotten anything from the safe house."

Lou took a deep breath and let it go. "Look, I believe you. But you have to bring more than a hunch to these folks. You've worked with them before. They're all about credible, solid evidence—otherwise they won't act."

Leine rose from her chair. "That's why I need to get moving."

"I'm here if you need anything." Lou stood. "Just let me know."

"Thanks, Lou. I appreciate it." He always had her back. They'd worked together a long time—knew each other's strengths and weaknesses, and trusted one another completely. In the world in which they operated having someone to trust was golden.

After Lou left, Leine slid on the ballistic vest and a T-shirt. Then she shrugged on the holster for the 9mm, concealing it with the leather jacket before she walked downstairs to meet her car rental agent. She'd requested a nondescript sedan, and that's what she got. The brown Hyundai's darkened windows were good for keeping the interior cool from the Southern California sun but also afforded Leine a bit of camouflage. And a brown sedan wouldn't be remarkable anywhere in California.

"Thanks for working late. I appreciate it." She gave the agent a credit card with a name that matched her passport and driver's license: Angela Holmes, 37, from Omaha, Nebraska.

"How long are you here in Los Angeles, Ms. Holmes?" asked the rental agent, obviously trying to be friendly.

"A week," Leine answered. She wasn't in the mood for friendly.

"Here on business?"

"Yes."

The agent got the message from her terse answers and stopped trying to make small talk. He gave her the receipt, wished her a good trip, and hopped in a car with the agency's logo on the side that was idling next to the Hyundai.

Once the agent and his driver had gone, she went back upstairs to retrieve the duffel bag, which she placed in the trunk. Then she got into the car and headed for the freeway. En route she dialed Recker.

"There's been some activity," he said when she asked. "One of the occupants left the premises and brought back several bags from a fast food joint." He paused for a moment. "There've been a couple of phone calls. One was at five twenty-six this evening, and sounded like someone was checking in. The other was definitely somebody with some clout. That one came in twenty minutes later. Dmitry took the call. I don't speak French, so I recorded his side of the conversation. I told Kathy. She's pretty good at translating."

"Is it accessible? I'm fluent in French."

"Yeah, it's on the cloud. I titled it using today's date and the time the call came in."

"What happened after the call?"

"An unidentified male asked Dmitry if it was the boss, and he confirmed that it was. When he tried to get more information, our guy shut him down, telling him he wouldn't need his services. Sounds like he's still waiting for a call back for the place and time."

"Anything else?" she asked. That meant there were at least three occupants in the safe house—the Russian, Dmitry, and an unidentified male.

"Negative. I'll give you a call if I hear anything. I've got another three hours before Miguel and Vernon come on shift."

"Thanks, Recker."

Leine ended the call. If it had been Salome, then all Leine would have to do was wait until Dmitry received the next call, and follow him to the meeting. If it had been someone else, then at least she'd be able to identify another operative in Salome's universe. Leine wondered if the terrorist knew she was in LA. If this was a trick to put her off the scent, then she did. If not, Leine might still have the element of surprise.

33

Santiago Jensen pulled his car to the curb and shifted into park. He glanced at the light shining from the porch of the restored bungalow and killed the engine. Heather had told him to go around to the back, that the door would be open and to just come on inside.

He wasn't sure why she called him to help her move her mother's armoire. She'd lived in LA for most of her life. Didn't she have other, younger friends who could do it? She was a surfer. Surfers were in great shape, generally. Not that Santa was in bad shape, but he felt like his moving days were in the rearview mirror.

With a sigh, he climbed out of the car, shut the door, and locked it. He liked the vintage Camaro—the manual door locks, the rumble of the big block motor, the feel of power in his hands. Leine had loved the car, too.

The long-buried memory of losing her hit him like a gut punch. She was everywhere. Places they'd been. Things she'd said. Even her scent—a touch of Chanel, the only perfume he'd ever seen her use. If someone walked by wearing that particular scent, for an instant he'd be overwhelmed by loss. The small reminders sidelined him when he least expected. His friend, Putz, told him it got easier with time, but Santa had never dealt with loss like this before and couldn't imagine it ever getting better.

Whenever he was hit with a reminder of her he'd berate himself. Leine wasn't dead. She was out there somewhere, breathing and living. He'd take solace in the fact that there was still the possibility of her. And then hope would raise its ugly head, and he'd have to bash it out of existence.

Pushing thoughts of Leine away, he walked across the street and up the driveway. It was a cool, clear night, although the stars weren't visible. That was one thing that irritated him about living in Los Angeles. Whenever he got out of the city and headed north, he was amazed at the brilliance of the stars. He had to remind himself that they were always there, even when he couldn't see them.

Like Leine.

Maybe it was time to move on. Find another place to live and work. A place without the constant reminders of everything he'd lost.

He skirted the house and stepped into the backyard. The porch light was on, but it didn't look like anyone was home—there were no lights on inside. Curious, he walked up to the door and knocked.

There was no answer.

Santa tried the door handle. It was unlocked, just like Heather had said it would be.

"Mrs. Brody?" he called, stepping through the doorway. Again, no answer. Heather hadn't mentioned her mother was hard of hearing, but it was a possibility. He moved farther into the house. "Heather?"

The place smelled of mildew and dust. Strange that a woman of means like Mrs. Brody didn't have a cleaning service.

Heather came from blueblood stock—her father had been a senator, and her mother an active philanthropist. When Senator Brody passed away, he'd left his wife and daughter with some hefty bank accounts.

He spotted a light switch and flicked it on, revealing a plain kitchen with white painted wooden cupboards. The counters and stove were clean but looked like they hadn't been used in a while. Something didn't seem right. Wary, he pulled his Glock from his shoulder holster and advanced into the living room.

"Anybody home?" His voice echoed back to him from the empty room. Did she give him the wrong address? That wasn't like Heather. He stopped and pulled his phone out of his pocket. He'd call Heather and find out what was going on.

The floor creaked behind him. Santa pivoted, gun in hand. *Thwop.* A hot jolt of pain seared his thigh, and his leg buckled like he'd been kicked by a mule. A moment later, something stung his neck. The sensation bloomed like fire.

What the—?

He clapped his hand against the pain and hit the dart. Brushing it away, he tried to raise the Glock in the direction of a backlit figure standing near the kitchen, but his arms felt like anvils and he struggled to aim. His vision began to cloud, and the room tilted.

Seconds later, the floor rocketed up to meet him. Santa collapsed, facedown, still gripping his gun.

34

Leine positioned her rental car out of sight of the safe house, down the block from where Recker had parked. The battery in the bug he'd planted on Dmitry at the airport had died, so he was using the parabolic mic to listen. He kept her updated on the conversations inside the house, but there hadn't been anything worthwhile to report. Meanwhile, she listened to the recording of Dmitry's side of the phone call, taking notes so she could refer back to what he said.

The one-sided conversation gave the impression that Dmitry was indeed speaking to someone higher up in the food chain, but there was no indication it was Salome. In fact, Dmitry was particularly cautious in his responses. Nothing important could be gleaned from the conversation.

Leine took a long pull on a bottle of water as she waited. She needed something concrete before her meeting with the feds the next day. Identifying a possible target would help with allocating resources, but she'd take anything that would make them sit up and take notice. Hopefully they'd deem the information credible and focus their considerable efforts on monitoring the safe house and its occupants.

"Sounds like Dmitry's on the move." Recker's voice broke into her thoughts. "He just asked the Russian for the keys to the SUV."

"Did he give them to him?" Leine asked.

There was a pause. "Yeah, he said he'd drive, but Dmitry shut him down. Told him to stay at the house until instructed to do otherwise. You should see him in a minute."

Leine waited until the SUV cleared the driveway and turned left before she started the car and followed.

"Let me contact Vernon and Miguel, see what their ETA is," Recker suggested. "If they're nearby, you can tag team him."

"Go ahead. But tell them to stay back in case he gets squirrelly again."

"Will do."

Leine kept far enough back so Dmitry wouldn't be able to ID her car but close enough so she could keep his taillights in view. The still-heavy rush hour traffic was a mixed blessing. On the one hand, it was good cover. One nondescript car in a sea of cars wouldn't be seen as an obvious tail. On the other hand, the SUV could be easy to lose in the sea of red taillights. And if he turned onto a sparsely traveled road, a pair of headlights behind him wouldn't be difficult to spot.

An hour later, Dmitry still hadn't done anything noteworthy. To anyone else, the guy appeared to be driving aimlessly, taking various off-ramps and cruising the odd neighborhood. To Leine, he was obviously looking for a tail. She employed every evasive maneuver she could think of to avoid detection and not lose the target. So far he wasn't acting like he'd spotted her.

"Hurry up, already," she muttered, drumming her fingers on the steering wheel. "You're not *that* precious." An hour in surveillance mode was two hours too long in LA traffic. She tamped down her annoyance and continued to drive. Vernon and Miguel offered to help, but Leine told them it wouldn't be necessary. *It's not like he's taking me anywhere.*

Grabbing the guy for an impromptu interrogation was beginning to look better and better.

Calm down, Leine. You're close. You know you are.

Her mobile buzzed. It was Lou. Letting loose a sigh of frustration, she answered.

"What've you got, Lou?" she asked.

"Heather Brody just called."

"Santa's partner?"

"Yeah."

Surprise at hearing Heather's name morphed into a sliver of alarm shimmying up Leine's spine. "Why?"

"She says Santa's missing."

"He's *what?*"

"He's missing. She hasn't heard from him and she's worried. She thought maybe you'd seen him."

The sliver of alarm became Def Con 1. Leine consciously loosened her death grip on the steering wheel. "What does his C.O. say?" He always notified his commanding officer if he was taking comp time.

"She says he hasn't heard from him either. They've alerted all patrols to be on the lookout."

"How long has he been gone?"

"Two days, maybe more. He was supposed to help her mother move an armoire a couple of nights ago, but he never showed. He's not answering his phone."

"Shit. This has Salome written all over it."

"You read my mind. What do you want to do?"

Def Con 1 had just turned into war. "I'll tell you what I'm going to do," Leine said evenly, her voice deathly calm. "I'm going to have a little talk with our friend, Dmitry. Right *now.*"

35

L eine's phone erupted for the fourth time with another call from Lou. She silenced her notifications.

Dmitry turned onto Mulholland Drive and began the climb up the famously winding street. *Perfect.* Leine knew the terrain from a job she'd done for SHEN several years before, when she helped take down a child sex trafficking ring headed by a well-known movie producer.

She kept just one car between them, not caring if he made her. Laser-focused on the SUV and her objective, Leine refused worry or fear a seat at the table in her mind. This was a fact-finding mission, plain and simple. She was going to get whatever facts Dmitry knew. It wouldn't be pretty, but that wasn't a problem as far as Leine was concerned.

Santa was in trouble. That was all that mattered.

The car directly ahead of Leine turned in to a driveway. Leine stayed back just far enough that it wouldn't make Dmitry skittish. Yet. They wound through the hills, their headlights illuminating worn asphalt and brush. Several switchbacks later, when Leine didn't turn off, Dmitry accelerated in an attempt to get some distance between them, but she matched his speed and maintained the same gap. The SUV sped up again, but the brake lights blinked on as he shut it down on the next hairpin turn.

He's getting nervous. A dark, unfamiliar road with an aggressive car on his ass.

She had his attention.

Dmitry sped along the next straightaway but slowed again as another sharp turn materialized in his headlights. Leine maintained her distance as they climbed, calmly thinking of what lay ahead. Far-off lights twinkled in the valley below. She eased her 9mm from her shoulder holster, screwed on the suppressor, and placed the weapon on the seat beside her.

They were close to one of the vista point turn offs, a section of road where people could pull to the side and view the city lights stretched across the valley like brilliant, glowing gems on a bed of concrete. She could bump him from behind, but that was a tricky move on a road with a steep drop. She didn't want him plummeting to his death.

At least, not yet.

The SUV's brake lights blinked on and Dmitry skidded to a stop on the pull out, making her decision for her. A cloud of dust overtook the vehicle. Leine was out of the car and headed for the SUV before the haze cleared. She slipped behind the back of the vehicle and stole along the passenger side. The reflection in the side mirror showed Dmitry glancing out the driver's side window, a pistol in his right hand. Leine stood back, aimed, and pulled the trigger.

The glass shattered and Dmitry screamed in pain as the bullet slammed into the back of his hand, carving a bloody hole through the delicate bones and embedding itself in the dash. Swearing a blue streak in Russian, his gun toppled to the floor. He wrenched the door open and half-slid, half-fell out of the SUV, scrambling to find his weapon with his left hand. Leine dropped to the ground and fired under the chassis, hitting him in the ankle. Dmitry grunted as his leg buckled and he dropped to the dirt.

Leine leapt to her feet and sprinted around the front of the SUV, keeping the engine block between her and Dmitry. She glanced over the hood. Grimacing in pain, Dmitry rocked back and forth, gripping his ankle and swearing under his breath. No gun was visible. She eased around the front of the vehicle, her pistol ready.

Dmitry's face contorted in anger. "What do you want?" he growled. His breath came in short gasps.

Leine circled around behind him, making sure he didn't have a weapon hidden behind his back. He didn't, although he most likely had something hidden somewhere. Dmitry swiveled his head, tracked her as far as he could.

Leine checked her car's position—she'd parked at a good angle, concealing Dmitry from passersby.

"Don't remember me, huh?" she asked.

Dmitry stopped rocking long enough to stare at her. Recognition lit his eyes. "The bitch who double-crossed Tsarev."

"Aren't we surly?" Leine motioned with her gun. "Move away from the door."

Dmitry didn't budge.

"Now." Leine walked up behind him and shoved him onto his side with her foot. His breath caught and he gasped in pain.

Keeping an eye on him in case he tried anything, she moved to the open door of the SUV and retrieved his gun from the floor mat and slid it into her waistband. Then she returned and patted him down, searching for other weapons. When she reached his good ankle, he grabbed her arm in a vise-like grip, his eyes narrow with rage. Leine dropped knee-first onto his injury and at the same time slammed her fist into his face. His head snapped backward.

Howling with pain, he let go of her wrist and shook his head to clear it. She was off him in an instant and resumed the pat down, liberating a small pistol from a concealed ankle holster. There wasn't anything else.

"What do you want?" Dmitry repeated, panting with the effort. Grimacing, he leaned back in the dirt. With his damaged right hand cradled against his stomach, he clutched his blood-soaked foot with his left. The blood seeping from the wound wasn't too bad, considering. Evidently the round hadn't hit an artery.

Keeping her distance, Leine dropped to her haunches and gazed at him for a moment, trying to determine what kind of inducement would work on him.

"You were in Chechnya." She seemed to remember Lou or somebody telling her he'd fought in the Chechen Special Forces before going freelance.

"What of it?" he asked. The grimace returned.

Leine shrugged. "No reason, really. I'm just establishing what kind of interrogation methods to use."

A look she couldn't read passed over his face. It wasn't fear or calculation. Relief?

She popped the locks on the doors to the SUV and walked to the rear cargo compartment, where she checked for supplies. There was a roll of duct tape, several plastic zip ties, some rope, and a box of plastic contractor bags. Everything a murderer would need. Or a terrorist. She moved the bags and rope to the backseat, then grabbed the ties and tape and walked back to Dmitry.

"Take your hand away," she ordered, gesturing to his foot. Dmitry narrowed his eyes but did as instructed. She wrapped the tape tight around his shattered ankle several times and zip-tied his hands behind his back. "Get up." With some difficulty, Dmitry climbed to his knees and then his feet. He stood with his weight on his good leg, favoring the injury. She shoved him toward the back of the SUV.

"Get in."

He hop-limped to the back and climbed inside. She zip-tied his ankles together, then shut the door.

With Dmitry safely stowed in the cargo area of the SUV, Leine went back to the driver's side, turned the key, and checked the fuel tank. It was three-quarters full.

She drove her car closer to the edge of the turn-off and killed the engine. Then she transferred the duffel bag, backpack, and extra bottles of water to the SUV. She slid Dmitry's gun into the backpack and swept the glass off the seat before she got in. Then she started the engine.

"Where are we going?" Dmitry sounded resigned.

"Somewhere more private."

She drove to a vacant lot in an industrial part of town, where no one would be working late. Dmitry tried to get her to talk on the way, but Leine stayed quiet. The less she said, the more of a game she could play with him. By the time they reached the vacant lot, Dmitry had stopped trying.

A good sign.

Leine parked and left the engine running. She grabbed her 9mm with the suppressor, her tactical knife, and the rope, and walked to the back of the SUV.

When she opened the door, Dmitry struggled to a half-sitting position.

"Slide this way," Leine ordered.

Watching her warily, Dmitry did as he was told.

Leine took one end of the rope and tied it around his ankles, making sure it was secure. Then she took the other end and looped it around the trailer hitch.

"What the fuck are you doing?" Dmitry asked. A mixture of alarm and anger laced his words.

The pistol in her hand, she motioned to him again. "Get out."

Slowly, Dmitry slid out of the cargo area and stood. He grimaced as he tested his weight on his wounded ankle and immediately shifted to the uninjured one.

"Okay," Leine began. "Now is when you tell me everything you know about Salome and her plans here in LA. Especially involving the homicide detective, Santiago Jensen."

Dmitry gave her a puzzled look. "I don't know what you are talking about. Salome? Santiago?" He shook his head. "I do not know these people."

Leine rolled her eyes. "Seriously? I don't have time for your bullshit. Tell me what you know, or you're going for a ride."

He remained silent, glaring at her from under hooded eyes.

She shrugged. "If that's the way you want to play it." She moved behind him and slammed her foot into the back of each knee. Groaning, he collapsed to the ground. Then she ripped off a piece of duct tape from the roll and slapped it over his mouth. She leaned down close to his ear and said, "I will do *everything* short of kill you, until you give me the information I need."

The tape muffled his response, but his intent was clear. He wasn't going to comply.

Leine walked back to the SUV, climbed in and put the vehicle in drive. She glanced in the rearview. "One last chance, Dmitry," she called.

He shook his head, defiant to the end.

She depressed the accelerator, and the SUV crawled forward. It would take a bit of time for the rope to play out. A moment later, the SUV balked ever so slightly from the added weight before continuing on its journey.

She inched forward, wanting Dmitry to get the full effect of gravel and broken asphalt ripping at the skin of his back. Not knowing how much torture he'd endured during the conflict in

Chechnya, she wasn't sure how much he'd be able to take. More than most, she'd bet.

When she didn't get a response, she checked the mirror to make sure the rope still held. Dmitry was several feet behind the vehicle, being slowly dragged along. Leine added more gas, and the SUV sped up. She made it to the end of the lot, turned right, and then shifted into park. She exited the vehicle and walked to the back of the SUV.

His shirt was bunched under his armpits, revealing a smooth, bare chest. Dirt and grime covered his clothes, and tears streaked his dirt-smeared face. Leine reached down and ripped the tape off his mouth.

"You crazy BITCH," he gulped. "I was screaming for you to stop." Dmitry bawled—great choking sobs—as Leine pulled him to a sitting position. The torn skin on his back was a mix of blood and gravel.

"Oops. My bad. I didn't hear you." She wasn't the least bit sorry. If it was the other way around—and it had been, in the abandoned warehouse in Athens—he wouldn't have shown any mercy. She leaned against the tailgate of the SUV and crossed her arms. "Where are they?"

Dmitry closed his eyes as though attempting to bring himself under control. The sobbing slowed. He took a deep breath and opened his eyes.

Through gritted teeth he said, "I don't know where Salome is, but I know where to find your detective."

36

S antiago Jensen raised his head slowly and opened his eyes. Jesus God, he was cold.

The icy fingers of bare concrete clawed his spine. Several pinpricks of light flickered in his periphery, casting a greenish hue on the floor.

Had he been sleeping?

No. He remembered now. The bungalow. His head throbbed like a wrecking ball had met the business end of a jackhammer, and his leg hurt like a mother.

One glance at his bloody thigh told him he'd been shot. The blood was caked and dry, suggesting that the bleeding had stopped. The numbness creeping up his legs was a blessing.

He moved his jaw back and forth, tasting the dusty gag in his mouth. His wrists were tied behind him with what felt like Flexi-Cuffs and attached to something hard and metal. He tested the strength of the cuffs, but the nylon ties cut into his wrists with each try. His ankles had been lashed together with the same ties. He tried to shift his weight to find a more comfortable position, but the floor was hard and cold no matter what.

He leaned his head back and assessed his surroundings.

Dark shapes lined the walls. A series of static green lights punctuated the darkness at intervals, suggesting some kind of electronics. The ceiling above him loomed black and featureless. Dust mixed with the distinct odor of singed plastic hung heavy in the air. There was no sound to speak of, other than the faint hum of a generator somewhere he couldn't see.

Santiago closed his eyes and thought back to his last memory. He'd gone to what he thought was Heather's mother's house to help her move a piece of furniture. He went inside, and that was the last he remembered.

Who would want to kidnap him? Could be someone he put in prison. The idea that someone would come find him, looking for revenge, had always been on a low simmer at the back of his mind, but he assumed if that happened the assailant wouldn't wait to smoke him.

This felt like something else.

Something worse.

C'mon, Santa. Don't let your imagination get the better of you.

As he contemplated his fate, a door at the back of the room clacked open. The gloom revealed the silhouette of a man moving toward him. The bright beam of a flashlight blinked on and illuminated the floor, highlighting several piles of cardboard and garbage swept to the side. When the man passed the center of the room, the flashlight briefly illuminated the source of the blinking lights. Santa tensed as a cold chill arced through his belly.

A series of rectangular boxes, all roughly the same size, sprouted colored wires from a smooth plastic housing. He caught a glimpse of a blank LED screen and a rudimentary switch.

Explosive devices. Lots of them. Beads of sweat broke out on Santa's forehead as the man approached.

He stopped a few feet from him and bent down, placing a

small tray on the floor. Using his foot, he slid the tray toward Santa.

"Dinner," the man grumbled.

Santa eyed the meal. Steam curled lazily from a ceramic bowl, bringing with it the scent of stewed beef and potatoes. His stomach growled. How long had it been since he'd eaten? A bottle of water glinted in the flashlight's glow. He looked up at the man to see if he could make out who he was. His face was still in shadow. Santa tried to say something.

The man leaned over and untied the gag.

"It's kind of hard to eat with my hands tied behind my back."

The man grunted as he dropped to one knee and picked up a spoon from the tray. He put the flashlight down and dipped the spoon into the bowl, bringing the stew to Santa's lips.

Santa ate hungrily, not sure when he'd see his next meal. He needed his strength if he was going to make it out of there alive.

And he was definitely going to make it out alive.

"Why am I here?" he asked in a conversational tone.

The man remained silent and continued to feed him.

Between bites, he tried again. "What's your name?"

Still nothing.

"That's a lot of IEDs over there. Aren't you afraid one of them might go off?"

That got the man's attention. The spoon stopped mid-air but then continued its trajectory toward Santa's mouth.

"You stop speaking now." The man's gravelly voice held an edge.

Santa pegged his accent as Eastern European. That narrowed things down. He'd put away maybe half a dozen Russians. The majority of his collars had been angry white guys.

"What part of Ukraine are you from?" If the guy was Ukrainian, then he might be intrigued that Santa could tell by his accent. If not, then he'd probably still get some kind of reaction.

He was right.

The man bristled. The temperature in the room dropped to subzero. "I do *not* come from Ukraine."

"Sorry, bud. I'm not very good with accents. You're Russian, then?"

The man nodded, relaxing a bit, "*Da.*" Using the spoon, he scraped the bowl and held it up to Santa's mouth.

Santa studied the Russian, still partially in shadow, as he swallowed the last of the stew. "Did I do something to piss someone off?" he asked. "Because, you know, that wouldn't be much of a stretch."

The man didn't react.

"Look," Santa continued. "Wouldn't you want to know why someone tied you up next to a bunch of bombs? Because, you know, that's a lot of firepower over there. Obviously, my days are numbered. The least you could do is tell me why."

The Russian grunted and held the bottle of water to his lips. "You are like goat."

Santa drank half the bottle before the guy pulled it back so he could speak. "A goat? What the hell does that mean?"

The Russian screwed the cap back on the bottle and set it aside. Then he climbed to his feet.

"You remember movie, *Jurassic Park*?"

"*Jurassic P*—" Then he got the reference. One of the scenes had a goat tethered to a rope to lure in T. rex. He glanced up at the Russian. "I'm being used as bait?"

"*Da.* Bait." With that, the Russian picked up the tray with the empty dishes and the flashlight and left.

37

Leine pulled up to the warehouse and killed the engine. The surrounding scrub oaks, sycamores, eucalyptus, and attending understory provided ample cover for the SUV. Moonlight glinted off the windshield of an old Ford truck parked in a gravel lot in front of the structure. Other than the lone vehicle, there wasn't anything else suggesting the place was occupied—no lights, no activity, nothing.

She studied the exterior, looking for the best way inside. Devoid of windows, the entrance sported a pair of double doors, probably steel, probably locked. There were no exterior lights except for a tall yard light illuminating the weed-choked parking lot. A metal ladder ran up the right side of the building leading to the roof. It looked like a possibility.

"You're sure this is the place?" she asked, glancing in the rear-view mirror.

There was movement in the cargo area as Dmitry struggled to sit up and look out the window. In a voice all kinds of weary he said, "Yes, yes. He is there."

"How many guards?"

"I don't know. Maybe three."

Dmitry had all but given up trying to remain silent when she asked questions. Dragging him around tied to the back of the SUV had put a damper on his bravado. Or maybe it was the gunshot wounds.

"Any cameras?"

"I don't know."

She hit the release for the tailgate and grabbed the roll of duct tape before she exited the vehicle and walked to the back. Dmitry narrowed his eyes and struggled to sit up, clearly expecting more punishment.

"I think you do. Let me ask again. Any cameras?" She slid the tactical knife free.

"Yes," he said through gritted teeth. Perspiration coated his face, glistening in the moonlight. "There is always one near the door, one inside, and one covering the back. There could be more."

"Good to know. You never answered me—is Salome here?"

"Maybe."

"So, three cameras, and three guards. Possibly Salome. Anything else I need to know?"

"When will you stop the pain?" Grimacing, he shifted his position.

"When I find Santa." Leine tore off a piece of tape and slapped it over his mouth. Then she ran the loose end of the rope through a metal tie-down in the floor, and up his back, looping it around his neck, effectively hog-tying him from neck to ankle.

"Be good," she said, and closed the door with a quiet *click*.

She grabbed her backpack and filled it with the flash bang grenades, ammunition, duct tape, and the rest of the rope. Then she slung the strap of the submachine gun over her shoulder, holstered the 9mm, and slid the tactical knife back into her ankle sheath. Extra magazines for both guns found a place in her cargo pockets. She slipped on the NVGs and adjusted them.

Lou had given her a hard time when he delivered the weapons stash, joking about starting a war. The plan had changed, but the objective was still the same. Find Santa before it was too late. Then find and kill Salome.

She just hoped she had enough firepower to get him out.

She went in low and fast, staying out of range of the alleged cameras. The NVGs helped. The eerie green landscape focused her. Dmitry could have been telling the truth, although she assumed he was just making shit up at this point to keep her from hurting him. She also assumed she was being set up. Trusting anyone involved with Salome was pointless. But she had to find Santa—had to make sure he was still alive—and the warehouse was her only lead. She'd find a way to get him out if he was there.

Her promise to herself was still intact—she wouldn't kill anyone who wasn't directly responsible for the crime. Dmitry would die—he fell into the responsible category when he joined forces with Salome.

But not until she achieved her objective.

She wound her way toward the warehouse through the brush and trees to the ladder attached to the side of the building. Pausing with her hand on the bottom rung, she listened for several seconds. The song of crickets filled the night air, covering her actions. But they also obscured the sound of an approaching enemy.

Not seeing or hearing anything suspicious, Leine began to climb.

When she reached the top, she pushed her pack onto the roof and pulled herself up to the flat surface. She paused to listen again. An owl hooted somewhere in the woods behind her.

Satisfied that she hadn't been seen, she lay prone and scanned the rooftop for access points. The ancient heating system looked way past its prime but could indicate a way forward, even though a newer HVAC system had been installed nearby. There was a rooftop access hatch that looked promising.

In a crouch, she moved to the heating mechanism. Upon closer inspection, it obviously wasn't an option. The system was no longer functional. Rusted metal had effectively sealed the unit closed. Maintenance had more than likely shut it down, replacing it with the newer HVAC system.

Leine moved to the hatch and tried lifting it by the handle. It wouldn't budge. The lock didn't look too complicated, so she removed her set of lock picks and went to work.

Five minutes later, the access door clicked open. Wary of the noisy hinges, Leine slowly lifted the metal hatch and propped it open. A ladder disappeared into the darkness below. She shrugged on the backpack and descended.

38

The roof access led to a catwalk high above the darkened interior. She scanned the room through the NVGs, noting a forklift and massive rows of shelves sporting cardboard boxes. A faint glow emanated beyond the shelves, and she padded silently along the metal walkway toward it. As soon as she reached the end of the shelving she slowed, her gaze focusing on the blinking lights surrounding a cleared space below. Wires sprouted from what looked like a series of timers, although the LEDs weren't lit up.

Explosives? Leine debated her options. She could leave and call the police, letting them know about the bombs, risking detonation with Santa still possibly inside, or she could continue her search for him, make sure he wasn't in the building, and then contact the authorities.

She chose the latter. Leine continued past the last of the shelving and was headed toward another ladder on the far wall when she stopped short. There was someone sitting on the floor below. The person's head hung down as though sleeping, his legs stretched out straight.

Her heart sped up as she quickly climbed down the ladder.

Keeping to the shadows, she ghosted across the expanse of concrete floor toward the mute figure. At her approach, the person raised his head. Glowing greenish-white eyes blinked at her. Heart in her throat, Leine lifted the NVGs out of the way.

Santa.

She rushed to him and pulled the duct tape from his mouth.

"Am I glad to see you," he whispered.

"Are you all right?" she asked in a low voice, sliding her knife from its sheath. She cut his ankles free, then reached around to release his wrists.

"I'm fine," he said. "You need to get out, now. It's a trap."

She helped him stand. "You're hurt."

"It's nothing."

"Doesn't look like nothing."

"Trust me."

Fine. "How many are there?"

"I've only seen one gunman," he said, rubbing his wrists to bring back the circulation. "A Russian. He said I was being used as bait. I didn't know for what until you showed up."

"Salome," Leine said.

Santa gave her a sharp look. Thankfully, he saved the recriminations. She knew full well what he was thinking. She thought the same thing—her obsession had led to his being captured.

"Can you walk?" She glanced at the bloodstain on his thigh.

"Like I said, I'm fine. Let's go." He took a step and his leg buckled. Leine grabbed his waist to steady him.

"Sure you are." She wrapped his arm around her shoulders. "Any idea how to get out of here?"

Santa nodded across the room at a set of double doors. "The guy came through the door over there. I don't know if it leads to an exit, though. How did you get inside?"

She nodded at the catwalk above them. "Access panel on the roof. Can you climb?"

"I can try."

Leine let her backpack slide to the floor. She reached inside and grabbed her phone and the flashbangs. "Give me Heather's number. And your CO."

He recited the numbers, and she texted their location and a terse explanation to both, making sure to mention the explosives. She ended with a request for backup. She pocketed both grenades, slid her phone into her back pocket, and unholstered the 9mm, which she gave to Santa, along with an extra magazine. Then she repositioned the MP5 so she could one-hand it.

They made their way toward the ladder at the far end of the warehouse as quickly as Santa could move. His expression remained stoic, but she could tell putting pressure on his leg cost him. Beads of sweat rolled down his face, and he clenched his jaw with each step.

They made it to the end of the room with only steps to go before a door behind them slammed open. Still holding on to Santa, Leine spun them around to confront the threat. The glowing green shape of a heavily armed man appeared in her night vision goggles. He crossed the floor toward them, shadowing the shelves for cover. Leine motioned for Santa to hold him off as she moved into a better firing position. Santa nodded, waited until the man was partially exposed and fired several shots, hitting him in the torso and shoulder. The gunman sank to his knees and toppled face-first to the floor.

Santa dove behind a stack of shelving as another gunman appeared behind him and returned fire. Leine squeezed the trigger on the MP5, riddling the man's chest with bullets. His body juddered from the impact, and his knees buckled as he slumped in a heap on the floor. Leine ejected the spent magazine and slapped in another.

"Let's go," she said, and wrapped his free arm around her shoulders.

Adrenaline spurring them on, they raced to the ladder. Santa gestured for Leine to go first, but she shook her head.

"I've got your back. Start climbing."

Santa grabbed the nearest rung and pulled himself up, using his good leg to hoist his body to the next. Leine was on the first set of rungs when the sound of footsteps echoed toward them.

Correction: more than one set. Two glowing green figures moved toward them. Both wore NVGs and carried what appeared to be automatic weapons.

She looked up to gauge Santa's progress. He was halfway to the catwalk. She gestured for him to keep going, then dropped back to the floor in a crouch. Scanning for cover, she moved behind a stack of pallets and slid the barrel of the MP5 through the slats.

The two gunmen split up and disappeared, putting a stack of shelves between them and their quarry. A moment later, one of the men emerged to Leine's right, his gun aimed at Santa. Leine pulled the pin on the flashbang and rolled it hard across the floor toward him. She closed her eyes and covered her ears as the grenade exploded. Opening her eyes, she moved closer and squeezed off a three-round burst, hitting him center mass. The gunman's momentum carried him two faltering steps before his body folded and he dropped to the floor.

The other gunman was nowhere in sight. Leine narrowed her eyes, searching for movement that would give away his position. The sound of Santa pulling himself up the ladder seemed over-loud. She took a deep breath to calm her pounding heart.

There was movement to her left.

Leine swung the barrel of the MP5 toward the second gunman just as the *pop!* of automatic gunfire exploded from his weapon. Bright muzzle flashes gave her his exact location and she squeezed the trigger of the MP5, shredding him with a barrage of bullets and stopping the attack. The man's weapon clattered to the floor, but he remained on his feet, swaying like wet laundry in a breeze. Then, as though someone cut the strings on a marionette, the gunman slumped to the floor.

Eyes on Santa, she sprinted to the ladder. Sliding the submachine gun behind her back, she grabbed on to the bottom rung and pulled herself up. "Are you all right?" she asked when she reached him.

He shook his head and nodded at his shoulder. Blood saturated his sleeve and ran down his arm, dripping from his fingers.

"I can't dress your wound up here. We need to get you down. You're in no condition to climb."

"Fuck," Santa said, gritting his teeth against the pain.

Threading her arm through the rungs on the ladder for stability, she levered him down. Near the bottom, he hung by his left hand and dropped to the floor, landing on both feet. His injured leg gave out. He staggered, catching himself before hitting the floor.

"Fuck," he said again, groaning as he straightened.

Leine bent down, slid her knife free, and set to work on the hem of his long sleeve T-shirt, cutting away a thick strip. He clenched his jaw as she folded it and placed it against his shoulder. She pulled the duct tape from her pack and wound it around the fabric. The blood loss slowed, but didn't stop completely.

"We have to get you to a hospital," Leine said.

Santa shook his head. "I'm a fucking train wreck, Leine. Leave me here. Get help. I'll hold off the bad guys however long I can until the cavalry arrives."

"Fucking train wreck or not, you're coming with me." Making sure Santa could stand by himself, Leine ran to one of the pallets and jammed her heel into the old wood, splintering it apart. She picked up two of the slats and sprinted back.

"What are those for?" he asked.

"A splint," she said. "I need you mobile."

She placed one slat on each side of his injured leg, then wrapped them with the tape.

"Let's see what's behind door number two." She grabbed his good arm and threw it around her shoulders. "Ready?" she asked. Santa nodded. They started toward the door the Russian had used. The distance between it and them was a chasm.

They reached the doorway after what seemed like an hour but was actually less than a minute. Leine tried the handle. It turned. She opened the door a crack. An empty hallway stretched in front of them. She opened the door wide and they moved through.

They'd made it a few feet when the sound of footsteps echoed toward them from the other end of the hallway. Leine pivoted and hustled Santa back through the door. She slid the flashbang grenade from her pocket, pulled the pin and waited, her finger on the release. As the first of the assailants rounded the corner, she tossed the grenade and looked away, covering her ears. The metal canister bounced and rolled down the hall. Seconds later, a bright light and an ear-splitting *bang* filled the space.

Leine raised the MP5 and sprayed the hallway with rounds, cutting down first one, then two gunmen. More footsteps and shouting could be heard behind them.

"Go!" Leine pushed Santa back into the larger room and slammed the door shut. Santa fired, destroying the door handle. Leine tried opening the door—the lock had jammed. They moved as one back to the center of the room, surrounded by the blinking lights of the IEDs.

Santa half-walked, half-hopped to one side of the space and took cover behind the forklift. Leine reloaded and sprinted to the other side, slipping behind one of the floor-to-ceiling shelves filled with dusty boxes. She slid two of the boxes aside, giving her a view of the room. Moments later two more gunmen appeared from a different direction, moving quickly, one searching high, one low. Leine waited until they were in range and dropped them both with two three-round bursts.

More muffled voices erupted as feet pounded toward them. She dropped back behind the shelf.

"Leine—look out!" Santa shouted.

She spun around.

A gunman was coming at her from behind. Santa fired and hit him in the back of the head. He face-planted into the concrete.

More shouting. Leine pivoted in place, raised the MP5, and exploded from behind the shelves, firing as she ran.

Two more gunmen fell. She stopped, straining to hear if more were on their way. There was no sound except for the ringing in her ears from the gunfire. Not seeing anyone else, Leine turned and sprinted back to where she'd left Santa. He stepped out from behind the forklift and was about to say something when a gunman appeared behind him, a pistol in his hand.

"*Get down!*" she yelled. Everything happened as if in slow motion: Santa turned and aimed his weapon. Leine raised the MP5 as the other man fired. Santa jerked as the rounds slammed into him. He sagged against the forklift, the pistol slack in his hand.

39

Rage and adrenaline fueling her, Leine let loose with the MP5 and cut the man down where he stood. She pivoted, looking for the next threat, but there was no one else. Lowering her gun, she raced back to Santa, slumped against the forklift. Blood poured from the wound. He clutched his arm, attempting to stanch the flow, but she could see he was fading fast. At least it wasn't pumping across the room, so his artery was intact.

Scarcely breathing, Leine cut a strip from the bottom of her T-shirt with her knife and used it as a tourniquet. She used the last of the tape to secure the material and stanch the flow of blood.

Santa's face was ghostly pale in the dim light. She felt his face and neck. His skin was clammy. She had to get him to a hospital, now.

A crackling sound erupted above them. Leine glanced up, searching for the source. A square speaker had been mounted above the door at the front of the room. The sound of someone slow-clapping echoed through the warehouse.

"Brava, Leine. Brava."

Leine froze at Salome's disembodied voice.

"It was a good try," she continued. "Really. You both should be commended. You've killed so many of my men." There was a long sigh. "Payment will be steep, I'm afraid. You two aren't going anywhere." Her voice held a note of triumph. "So I've finally caged the Leopard. How does it feel to be experiencing your last few moments together?"

Leine propped Santa against the forklift. Panting from the effort to stand, he sagged against the machine and ejected his pistol's empty magazine. He then used his good arm to slide a new magazine from his pocket and reload.

Salome continued. "Why did you wait so long to come back to the United States? One would think you'd want to be in Los Angeles, of all places. Your daughter is here. Your detective is here. Your employer is here. And now, so is your dirty little street urchin."

Leine's heart rate quickened. *How does she know about Jinn?* No one knew where she was except Lou, his wife, and Jessica, the woman who traveled to Los Angeles as Jinn's chaperone. SHEN had vetted Jessica extensively before allowing her to accompany a minor abroad. Nigel Cripps knew the location of the foster parents, but not what happened to Jinn.

"Yes, I know she didn't die in the explosion at the museum." Salome's voice sounded bored. "For someone who was once an elite assassin, you should really try to cover your tracks better."

Jinn had traveled under an assumed name, and Leine was absolutely certain no one followed her to the airport to drop the kid off. Was it possible that Jinn's foster parents had been compromised? It didn't make sense. Nigel assured both Lou and Leine that they were well hidden.

"What do you want, Salome?" Leine asked, suddenly weary of playing cat and mouse.

"What do I *want*?"

Leine rolled her eyes at the dramatic incredulity in her voice.

"What do I *want*?" she repeated. "I *want* you to stop breathing. I *want* you to stop ruining my *life*." She paused for a moment before continuing. "You're predictable, Basso. I once toyed with the idea that you and I were destined to work together. To forge an unstoppable duo of powerful, feared, and respected women who were at the top of their game. But you showed me time and again that was not to be." Another long sigh. "Pity. We could have achieved so much more together."

"You say you know me. You don't." Leine slid the NVGs down and scanned the room, searching for cameras. *There.* Why hadn't she seen it before? A camera had been mounted on one of the upper shelves, giving it a bird's-eye view of the cleared space with the explosives. She raised her gun and fired. Shattered glass pinged the floor.

One down.

"Shoot all of the cameras. It won't do you or your lover any good. Did you notice the explosives? I expect there won't be enough of either of you left for identification. Besides, your detective looks as though he won't be with us much longer."

Leine checked her watch. Fifteen minutes had elapsed since she'd sent the texts to Heather and Santa's CO. She needed to keep Salome talking, stall for time.

"So all the subterfuge with the Bomb Maker and Edinburgh and Dmitry—all that was simply to play me?" Leine asked. "Seriously, Salome. All you had to do was tell me you were in Los Angeles. I would have been here as soon as I could book a flight."

"Oh, I doubt that. You were *obsessed* with finding me, but you needed to feel as though you did it on your own, didn't you? Admit it. It was such fun playing with you for so long." Salome's laughter sounded distorted over the PA system, like it was being piped in from all directions in a carnival fun house.

"You overestimate me, Salome. I don't need to be the one to track you down. I'd be happy no matter how you died."

"I am afraid you will have to wait for that seminal event. I suspect you will experience the other side long before I do." There was a pause. "You have two minutes to say goodbye to your detective. Starting now."

At that moment, each of the individual LED screens attached to the explosives blinked on, flashing two minutes in glowing red.

The numbers began to count down. 1:59...1:58...1:57...

They had to try. Leine grabbed Santa's good hand and was about to wrap his arm around her shoulders when a glint of metal on the forklift's console caught her eye.

The key.

"Help me get you onto the forklift," she whispered. Pushing Santa as far onto the floor of the forklift as possible, she raced to the other side and climbed onto the seat. She took a deep breath, turned the key, and pressed the start button. The engine turned over, but didn't catch. The second try produced the same result.

Leine closed her eyes and tried again.

The engine caught, coughed several times, and rumbled to life. She threw the shifter into reverse, spun the steering wheel 180 degrees, and rammed the accelerator to the floor.

The hulking forklift was surprisingly quick. They covered the expanse of floor in seconds, headed for an outside wall.

At the last minute, she threw the gear shift into neutral and braked hard. She jumped to the floor and ran to Santa to help him from the forklift.

"Can you stand?" she asked.

Though he appeared shaky, he waved her off. "Yeah. Do it."

Leine picked up a loose slat from a pallet on the floor, ran back to the forklift, and climbed onboard. She wedged the piece of wood between the accelerator and seat. The engine whined as it revved, fighting to get loose.

Then she slammed the machine into reverse.

Leine leapt off the forklift as it rocketed backward, headed for the wall. Seconds later, the machine slammed through the concrete blocks with an enormous *bang!* Leine dragged Santa through an opening in the bent rebar and over the pile of rubble as the explosives detonated.

40

S irens.

Ears ringing, Leine opened her eyes. She stared upward, trying to remember where she was. Brilliant white stars punctuated the cold, black sky above her, matching the chill of the ground. The scent of damp earth and dead leaves brought her back to the present.

October. Los Angeles. Santa.

Salome.

Deep breaths. The coughing fit racked her body in waves. Slowly, she raised her head. The world around her spun.

Taking another deep breath, she pushed herself to a sitting position. The spin lessened.

The cinderblock wall of the warehouse stood in ruins a few feet from her. The large opening resembled the jagged, crenelated wall of a castle—the roof she'd been on not an hour before had been obliterated. Flames danced along scattered pieces of pallet wood. Engine still running, the forklift had continued its trajectory until it wedged against the base of a scrub oak.

She swiveled her head, searching for Santa. There was something in the underbrush and Leine crawled toward it.

Let him be alive.

He was lying facedown in a pile of fallen leaves at the base of an old pin oak. Leine felt his carotid artery and sighed with relief at the pulse pushing beneath her fingers. She checked what areas she could for additional injuries before rolling him onto his back and brushing the dirt and leaves from his face.

"Santa," she said, patting his face. "Santa, wake up."

The sirens were getting louder. Leine raised his head, cradling it in her lap.

He groaned and tried to sit up.

"Shh," she soothed. "Stay put. The ambulance will be here soon."

"Salome?"

Leine shook her head. "I don't know."

"She knows about Jinn..." He tried to sit up again but then thought better of it and sank back into her lap. "And probably April. You need to stop her."

She slid her phone from her back pocket. The cracked screen resembled a spider's web. "Shit." She tried calling Lou. There was no response. "The phone's dead."

"Go. I'll make sure they know about April and that you need backup."

"I can't leave you." Her throat closed and she blinked back tears, surprised at the force of her emotions. *It's the adrenaline,* she thought.

"Yes. You can." This time he managed to raise himself onto his elbow. The pained look on his face told her it cost him. "I'll be fine. Help will be here soon."

"No," she said. What if he died? She couldn't live with herself.

But what if Jinn or Lou or Nita died? How will you live with yourself then?

"Go. I'll be fine."

Leine warred with herself a few moments longer. Knowing he was right, she took off her jacket and folded it in fourths. Carefully, she moved out from under him and laid him down, his head resting on her jacket.

She found Dmitry's pistol inside the backpack and holstered the semiauto. She rose to leave and Santa grasped her hand. She hesitated. He captured her fingers and brushed his lips across her knuckles. Leine closed her eyes and after a brief moment slid her hand free.

With one last look, she picked up the pack and started back toward Dmitry and the SUV. She'd made it about twelve yards when a figure appeared from behind the trunk of a gnarled manzanita.

She stopped, automatically reaching for her gun.

"Leine?" Heather Brody strode toward her.

Leine relaxed and let her hand drop to her side. Good. Someone to look after Santa.

"I got your text. What the hell happened?" Heather scanned the area behind Leine. "Where's Santa?"

"Back this way about a dozen yards," Leine replied, turning toward where she'd left him. "He's hurt and needs immediate attention. I'll show you."

When Heather didn't follow, Leine glanced behind her. The other woman's service pistol gleamed in the moonlight.

"What are you doing?" Leine's heart rate ratcheted up as another surge of adrenaline kicked in. She considered reaching for the pistol, but Heather would be one step ahead.

Leine was fast, but not that fast.

Heather's eyes glistened with unshed tears. "They know everything."

Leine raised her hands, hoping to calm the other woman. "You don't have to do this, Heather. Whatever it is, we can work it out."

"I'm sorry..." Heather raised her gun.

Leine dove for the ground and rolled, and at the same time yanked Dmitry's pistol from her holster. She leapt to her feet as a gunshot cracked through the still night air. Leine braced for the searing pain of a gunshot wound.

It never came.

Heather sucked in a sharp breath and clutched her stomach. The surprise on her face turned to stunned disbelief as she looked down at the blossoming red stain on the front of her shirt. Her gaze met Leine's and her knees buckled. She wavered for an instant before falling sideways onto the damp ground, still clutching her gun.

Leine looked back to where she'd left Santa. He leaned against the oak tree, his expression a mixture of resignation and anguish. He held his injured arm flat against his torso, blood saturating his shirt.

In his other hand was the pistol she'd given him earlier.

"Go," he called to her, his voice weak. "Before it's too late."

Leine picked up the backpack and ran.

Spencer Simms waited for the Accountant under the same bridge as before. He'd never left London, only told Leine he was in Paris. He had to stay—otherwise he wouldn't be able to finish what he started.

What began as a cold drizzle had turned into a steady rain, and he shrugged deeper into his coat. Not for the first time he wondered if he should have gone to Los Angeles. He'd be more effective if he was there.

Like Edinburgh?

Simms shook his head. What a clusterfuck that had been. Leine was even more suspicious of him, if that were possible. He sighed, checked his phone. The Accountant was due any minute.

At that moment, a dark figure crossed the cobblestone street toward him. Simms recognized the round glasses and self-important air of the reprehensible man. He drew his pistol and hid it in the folds of his coat. Then he tapped "record" on his phone and slipped it back into his pocket.

Better safe than sorry.

The Accountant slowed his approach, his hand in his pocket. Simms tensed and gripped the gun tighter. The other man withdrew a pack of cigarettes and shook one free.

"What is so important that it couldn't wait until morning?" The Accountant's lighter flared in the gloom. The flame reflected in his glasses, reminding Simms of a photograph he once saw of the head of the Gestapo, Heinrich Himmler. The other man put the lighter away and took a deep drag, the lit end of the cigarette glowing.

"I wanted to give you and your employer the chance to set things right."

The Accountant scoffed. "Please don't refer to her as my employer." A look of distaste came over his features. "We're partners."

"Oh, do forgive me. I meant your *partner*."

"And just what do you mean, set things right? As far as I'm concerned, everything is in order."

Simms moved closer to him so he wouldn't have to shout over the pounding rain.

"The money."

The Accountant waved his hand. "You've been paid. I told

you last time, we'll call you if we need you." He took another hit off his cigarette. "You've wasted my time." He turned to go.

Simms brought the gun up and aimed it at the other man. "You need to explain to me how you were able to track the Libyan girl to Los Angeles."

Eyeing the barrel of the gun, the Accountant threw his cigarette to the ground. The glowing red end fizzled with a spatter of rain.

"I didn't know you were so attached." He faced Simms, his hands at his sides where Simms could see them. "We have contacts."

"In British intelligence." It was a statement, not a question.

The Accountant cocked his head. "You've been busy."

"Not as busy as you, apparently."

"Look, I'll be happy to put your name forward if you're interested in joining our little group."

Simms chuckled. "Not necessary." He nodded at his gun. "It seems I have the upper hand at the moment. What do you have planned for the Basso woman?"

"You already know that."

"You misunderstand. What *exactly* do you have planned for her? Times, dates, places."

"I have no idea what you're talking about."

Simms sighed. "I'm not in the mood for your games. Tell me what I want to know and I may let you live."

The Accountant snorted. "Really? Afraid I can't tell you that, old man. It's hush-hush, you know. Eyes only. That sort of thing."

He doesn't know. "Compartmentalization. One cell doesn't know what the other is doing."

"Exactly. Each plays their part."

"Then I need to see your identification."

"My—" The man's expression became guarded. "I didn't bring it."

"Wrong answer." Simms raised the gun, aiming at his head. "I already know who you are. I would like you to verify."

"Oh, for fuck's sake." The Accountant rummaged in his coat pocket. "I'm going to call Salome. She'll vouch for me."

"That won't be necessary. Tell me your name."

"My name." The blank look on his face told Simms he wasn't used to being questioned.

"Yes, your fucking name. Starts with an N, doesn't it?"

"How did you—"

"That's not important."

Beads of sweat had formed on the sides of the Accountant's face. He wiped his brow. "Look. I have access to a large sum of money. Huge."

"That's lovely, really. But I don't need money."

"Then what are you getting on about?" The other man's eyebrows dipped in annoyance as he spread his arms wide. "You're not interested in working for me, not interested in money. Spell it out."

"I want you to say your name. For the record."

The Accountant sighed. "Fine. It's Nigel."

"Nigel..."

"Nigel Cripps." Cripps stuffed his handkerchief back in his pocket. "Satisfied?"

Simms nodded. "Yes, I am." He pulled the trigger, sending two rounds into Nigel Cripp's forehead. The echo of the gunshot was lost in the driving rain.

Simms rummaged through the dead man's pockets, retrieving a cell phone and wallet, and ripped the ridiculous beard and mustache from his face. He took out his own phone and snapped Nigel's photograph. The image wasn't very flattering—he'd landed faceup in a nasty puddle of brackish water, two round dark holes between his wide, unseeing eyes—but it would do.

He selected a number from his list of contacts and texted the picture, before picking up the brass casings.

A moment later, he was gone.

41

Leine slowed as she approached the SUV, MP5 aimed at the vehicle. The hood canted at a slight angle, evidence of a flat front tire. In a crouch, she skirted the side, listening for movement, wondering if Dmitry had survived his wounds. Not hearing anything, she eased around to the shattered passenger window and glanced inside. Nothing. She walked to the back. Standing to one side, she opened the door to the cargo area.

Dmitry lay with his back to her, the rope still intact. Leine raised the MP5 but hesitated. "Get up," she said, and prodded him with the barrel. He didn't respond. She grabbed him by the shoulder and rolled him onto his back. His mouth gaped open, his gaze fixed on the roof.

A deep red line arced across his throat. Ligature marks, most likely from a garrote. Blood soaked his neck and the top of his shirt. He hadn't been dead long.

Salome.

She dragged him from the back of the SUV and left him on the ground as she did a quick scan of the undercarriage, motor, and under the dashboard.

No explosives. She slid underneath and scanned the brake lines, but they were dry and intact.

Salome hadn't taken time out of her busy schedule to try to kill Leine on the road. That meant she had other plans. The flat tire was only meant to delay her. She could have shot two and left Leine stranded.

Leine dug out the spare and proceeded to change the tire. Salome had used a high-caliber round to get the job done. She finished as quickly as she could and returned the jack and the ruined tire to the cargo area.

Leine closed the back of the SUV and climbed behind the steering wheel.

She checked the time on the dash. Depending on traffic, she would be able to get to Lou's in forty-five minutes or less. Leine couldn't be sure how much of a head start Salome had on her, but anything was too much.

She raced to the freeway and mashed the accelerator to the floor, headed toward Lou's. She had to make it in time.

Images of Santa flashed through her mind. He'd lost a lot of blood.

He's going to be all right. You did the best you could to protect him and April.

April. Fear wound its tentacles around her heart. *She's got round-the-clock security. She's going to be all right.*

She had to be.

THE HOUSE WAS QUIET. A DIM LIGHT GLOWED FROM A FIRST-FLOOR window, but from what she could see, no one appeared to be inside. Salome checked the time. It was after eleven. Perhaps the occupants were already in bed.

She gave a wide berth to the home, avoiding the sliding glass doors that led to a daylight basement. Large picture windows on the upper level looked out on the fenced backyard. Knowing the kind of people the organization often came up against, she assumed the director of SHEN had installed security lights and cameras.

No matter. Salome knew how to circumvent security.

The detective was as good as dead, if he wasn't already. Unfortunately, the Basso woman had survived the blast. Once she'd seen what Salome had done to Dmitry, Leine would know she was on her way to kill the rest of her loved ones and would come to their aid.

Predictable.

After all the months of planning, of discovering what drove Basso, Salome's brief moment of self-doubt when her enemy had survived the blast didn't last long. After reworking her plan, she realized it would all come together even better than she'd thought. She'd killed her lover. That alone would leave a gaping emotional wound. Now that Basso knew Salome had found where they were keeping the child, it would only be a matter of time before the former assassin came to the rescue.

It was perfect, really. And Salome had the element of surprise. Basso may know she was there, but she'd be going in blind.

Then, after she killed Basso, she'd go after the daughter and anyone else the Leopard ever cared for. Pity she couldn't do it in front of her, but Salome had grown tired of playing the game.

Planning and executing their deaths would be a most enjoyable pastime and something she could accomplish between jobs for the Kremlin. Now that she and the Bomb Maker had relocated to the US, there'd be no stopping them.

42

Eyes glued to the console, Jinn sat cross-legged in a beanbag chair and obliterated the alien. A glowing green cloud appeared awarding her the points she needed to level up, and she suppressed a shout of joy so she wouldn't wake Lou and Nita, sleeping upstairs. Just then, a frighteningly huge cyclops materialized. Before the monster could destroy her character and end the game, she set her avatar loose.

She cued up her most powerful weapon and was about to deploy when the lights flickered and everything went dark. Jinn groaned and wrenched off her headphones.

"Not now, not *now*," she pleaded. Would the game even remember she'd leveled up? She'd been playing every chance she got, trying to beat the gamer nicknamed *TheBeast* out of Barcelona but hadn't been able to catch up to him. Tonight was the first time she'd come close in a week, and now she'd probably have to qualify *again*. She stared dejectedly at the blank screen, willing the program to come back online.

Please...please...please.

As though hearing her thoughts, the lights blinked on and the monitor flickered to life. The game had reset to her last level.

"No, no, no," she moaned. She dropped the controller to the floor beside her and crossed her arms in defeat. There was no use trying again tonight. It was getting late, and she was tired. She needed to be fresh for her next attempt. With a sigh, Jinn turned off the monitor, then stretched and yawned, and climbed to her feet. She'd get a good night's sleep and try again tomorrow. Conjuring an imaginary alien, she did a couple of moves she'd learned in kickboxing class, then switched off the light and padded upstairs.

The kitchen was eerily quiet, like the house had forgotten to breathe. There was only the faint buzz of the refrigerator and the occasional creak of a house settling on its foundation. Jinn enjoyed being the only person awake at this hour—it reminded her of when she used to walk through the medina late at night and listen to the ghosts, or jinns, that haunted the narrow corridors. That had been where the shopkeepers had given her the nickname Jinn of the Marketplace. She'd been like a ghost then, a spectral being, capable of appearing and disappearing when least expected.

As she walked toward her room, the little hairs on the back of her neck prickled. She slowed her pace, her senses alert. Something was off. Whether it was a scent, or a sound, or a feeling, she couldn't say, but something was wrong. After living alone for over two years on the streets of Tripoli, Jinn had learned to trust her instincts. Her feelings and senses had kept her from danger.

Her nostrils flared, and she took in a breath. That was it—an unusual smell. Different from Lou's or Nita's scent, or the scent from the vase of flowers on the dining room table. Different from the onions and garlic from dinner.

Tensing, Jinn slowed her breathing and stilled, listening. At first there was nothing but the normal sounds of a house at rest. The heater kicked on, and Jinn's heart leapt. She clamped her mouth shut, determined not to give away her position in case someone was in the house. Her fists clenched, she slipped behind the doorway and scanned the living room.

A dark shadow slid across the hallway on the far side of the room. Frozen in fear, Jinn squinted in the darkness, trying to make out what it was.

Had the jinns from the medina followed her to America? That couldn't be. The spirits she'd heard of and thought she'd seen there were rumored to be partial to Libya—especially the old medina. This house was too different than what they were used to—too modern. If there were spirits here, which Jinn fervently believed, they would be native to the area.

Even though she had worked diligently to attract them, she'd yet to see one.

Convinced that what she saw wasn't a house spirit, Jinn slipped back into the kitchen—her stocking feet silent on the tile floor—and hesitated near the stove, heart thudding in her chest. Half a dozen steak knives, a knife sharpener, and a 10-inch chef's knife protruded from a wooden block on the counter. Keeping an eye on the doorway, Jinn slid the chef's knife free and dropped down to her haunches. Then she closed her eyes to listen.

The heater fan stopped, plunging the rest of the house into silence. There was a whisper of sound to her left, and she opened her eyes. A dark shape moved past, headed for the hallway leading to Lou and Nita's bedroom.

A low growl started deep within Jinn's chest. Without thinking, she leapt forward, knife poised to strike. The shadow dodged the attack but not before the blade hit home. *It's human,* thought Jinn with a start. The person sucked in a sharp breath and yanked the knife from Jinn's grasp. Jinn backed up and turned to run, but the intruder caught her arm in an iron grip.

"Not so fast," a familiar voice hissed.

Jinn struggled against her captor, but the grip only tightened.

"Stop, or you die."

Jinn stopped struggling, searching her memory for a face to go with the voice. When it came to her she froze. She craned her neck to look at her captor. It was the woman terrorist. The one from Paris. Memories of being wired into a suicide vest came back with a vengeance, and her knees began to shake.

A door slammed open on the far side of the house, spilling light into a far hallway. Footsteps rushed toward them. The terrorist wrapped her forearm around Jinn's neck and dropped to one knee. The cold steel of the chef's knife pressed against her throat. Dressed in an oversize white T-shirt, Nita burst into the kitchen, a pistol in her hand.

"Don't come any closer, or the child dies," the woman said. The casualness of the delivery chilled Jinn to her bones.

Nita stopped short. "Don't hurt her." She looked at Jinn. "Are you all right?"

Too afraid to answer, Jinn gave a quick nod.

"Put the gun on the floor and kick it toward me."

"Just don't hurt her," she said again. Nita placed the gun on the floor and straightened.

"Kick it across the floor," the woman repeated.

Nita did as instructed.

"Where's your husband?"

"He's not here," Nita lied.

"Don't lie to me."

"I'm not—I wouldn't't."

The terrorist sighed. "He's here." She pressed the knife more deeply into Jinn's neck. Jinn sucked in a breath, afraid to swallow lest the blade slice her throat.

Nita raised her hands, pleading. "Please. She's just a child."

"Then tell me the truth. Where is your husband?"

The older woman's shoulders dropped in defeat. "He's outside. He thought he heard something."

"Good answer." The woman eased the pressure of the knife against Jinn's throat. Grateful for the reprieve, Jinn swallowed.

Nita hesitated. "If you already knew, then why ask me?"

"I wanted to make sure you would tell the truth." Her icy tone cut through the room.

"Is he—is he all right?"

"That depends on your perspective." The woman removed her arm from Jinn's throat and shoved the girl toward Nita. Jinn ran to the older woman.

"Sit down." The terrorist gestured toward the kitchen table as she bent to retrieve Nita's weapon. She opened a drawer and shoved the knife inside, then slammed the drawer shut.

Nita and Jinn sat down.

"Hands where I can see them."

Jinn and Nita placed their hands flat on the table.

"Who are you?" Nita asked. "And why are you here?"

The woman shook her head. "You'll know soon enough." She reached into the side pocket of her cargo pants and pulled out a handful of plastic ties, which she slid toward her. "Put these around the urchin's ankles and attach her to the chair legs."

Nita bent to do as she instructed. The other woman flicked on the stove light and came around the table to watch.

"Tighter."

Nita ratcheted the plastic ties around Jinn's ankles.

"Now her hands."

The older woman did as she was told.

"Good. Now do the same to your ankles."

Nita picked up one of the ties. Her gaze dropped to the other woman's bloody thigh. "You're hurt."

Jinn glanced at the woman's leg. A slice in the fabric sported a dark stain saturating her pant leg. *Good. I cut her.*

"It's nothing," the woman said. "Tie yourself."

Nita bent over in her chair.

"Faster," the woman scolded, and cuffed her across the back of her head with her gun, stunning the older woman.

"Don't hit her," Jinn shouted. Rage boiled inside of her at the sight of her friend being hurt.

"If you aren't quiet, you tiny shit, I'll do worse."

Jinn clamped her mouth shut as Nita did as she was told.

After she finished binding Nita's wrists to the chair behind her, the woman walked to the kitchen sink, where she soaked a towel she found hanging on the oven door, and used it to sponge off her leg. She rummaged through the drawers and pulled out another, which she ripped into strips to use as a tourniquet.

"You never answered my question," Nita said. The other woman shot her a look. "About who you are and why you're here."

"I'm here for a friend of yours." The woman glanced at the time on the microwave. "She should be here soon."

Jinn looked up at Nita, searching the older woman for a clue as to whom the friend might be. Did this horrible woman know Nita and Lou from somewhere?

Nita's body tensed. "Who *are* you?" she asked again.

"Call me Salome," she said, looking at Jinn. "And I'm here for Leine Basso."

43

L eine scanned the grounds of the house through binoculars, searching for signs of forced entry. Nothing looked disturbed. Did she make it in time?

She chided herself for wishful thinking.

After getting a visual on the hidden security cameras Leine installed for Lou three years ago, she located the motion sensor lights. All appeared intact. She reminded herself of their range and where she'd built in blind spots in case Lou ever found himself in trouble. Local law enforcement had copies of the security schematics so would know where to breach in case Lou's home was ever compromised, like now. If someone cut power to the home, the backup generator would resume in ten seconds, powered by a propane tank hidden in a garden shed next to the house. She just hoped Santa got the message to the right people and they came in quietly.

Bulletproof glass and steel doors kept the rest of the structure relatively safe, but there was always a way to outwit security protocols, depending on the assault. That was why Leine had insisted Lou install a panic room. He'd balked at her suggestion but finally relented. He'd received death threats over the years from some nasty characters, and his concern for his wife helped seal the deal. Now that Jinn was part of the family, that panic room was even more important.

A faint light glowed from the kitchen upstairs. In a normal scenario, that might've meant a late-night snack. Not this time. Just as she was about to leave her position, the light blinked out.

Leine slipped the binoculars into her pack and pulled her watch cap low on her forehead. She'd smeared her face with dirt which, combined with her black clothing, helped her blend into the shadows surrounding the house. Staying low, she skirted the yard, avoiding both the cameras and the motion sensor lights.

She made it to the garden shed and slipped inside. The sound from the propane tank told her the backup generator was in use.

She's already inside.

A digital lockbox that resembled an electrical outlet had been mounted on the wall next to the propane tank and contained a key to the front and back doors. Leine punched in the code and the box opened. She took the key and put it between her teeth, then slid Dmitry's semiauto from her holster, wishing again for another flashbang grenade. She didn't have time to resupply, and all she had left were binoculars, the night vision goggles, the pistol, an extra magazine, and her tactical knife. The MP5 was out of ammunition, or she would have brought that, too.

She turned off the propane and stepped from the garden shed. The rest of the house, including appliance LED lights, would go completely dark in a few seconds if it hadn't already, announcing her arrival. But coming through any of the doors or windows would have, too. This way, Salome wouldn't be sure where she entered.

Besides, she already knew Leine was coming for her.

Leine made her way up the gradual incline of the side yard

and rounded the corner of the garage. The key worked for the side door as well as the main entrance. She unlocked the door and eased it open.

Lou's white four-door pickup and a dark sedan were parked side by side, taking up most of the space. Tidy shelves lined one wall, and a work bench stretched across another. She stepped inside and stilled.

Drip.

Drip.

The sound diverted her attention, and she moved between the two vehicles, looking for the source. She ran her hand along the rim of the pickup bed, stopping at a small pool of something dark, and glanced up.

Her breath caught.

Lou.

The director for SHEN hung above her from the rafters, facedown and spread-eagled with his eyes closed, dripping blood from what appeared to be a gash in his torso. A rope ran from wrist to wrist and ankle to ankle, then wrapped around his midsection, before being used to hoist him to the ceiling. Heart thudding, Leine raced to cut him free. Using her tactical knife, she sawed through the nylon and lowered him gently to the floor.

"Lou," she whispered, checking his wound. The gash was close to three inches long. Leine eased the pickup door open and reached into the console for Lou's first aid kit. Finding what she needed, she packed the wound with gauze and wrapped his torso to stop the bleeding.

"Lou, wake up. It's Leine."

Lou's eyelids fluttered and he groaned. Blood soaked the area adjoining the gash, but appeared to have slowed from the wound itself.

"Come on, Lou."

The door to the house opened and closed. Leine tensed and eased her suppressed pistol from its holster. Measured and unhurried footsteps walked toward the pickup and then stopped. Leine repositioned the NVGs, rendering her surroundings green.

Lou started to say something, but Leine put her hand to his lips. His eyes flickered open, and she shook her head. He gave her a single nod and closed his eyes.

The intruder moved to the front of the pickup. Leine tracked the sound with the barrel of her gun.

Just one step closer.

The footsteps paused and then changed direction, walking around the opposite side of the truck. Leine leaned back so she had a visual of the underside of the chassis and waited, willing the other person to walk past the wheel well, giving her a target.

The footsteps paused again before backtracking toward the door. Leine sat up and moved into a crouch.

"Salome," Leine called. The footsteps stopped. Leine slipped behind the truck bed, staying low.

Something moved in her periphery and she turned. Flashes lit up the garage as three rounds slammed into the wall, just missing her. Leine returned fire. It was Salome. Her opponent ducked behind the pickup, her footsteps echoing across the confined space. Leine strode forward, firing multiple shots as she did. The rounds chewed up the trim around the door and embedded themselves into the surrounding drywall. Except for one. There was a gasp, and the door to the house slammed open. Leine sprinted past the pickup, racing to finish the terrorist off.

But she was already gone.

44

L eine ejected the spent magazine and slapped in the last full one she had. Fifteen rounds.

It had better be enough.

She jacked a round in the chamber and took a deep breath.

Adrenaline pumping, Leine eased into the house. Lou would be all right for the time being. He was awake and alive, and she'd done all she could.

He'd understand.

She glanced down and moved slowly, following the blood spatters on the floor. The door to the garage opened directly into a laundry room. One of the cupboard doors hung open, revealing a stack of folded towels. Leine crossed the room and paused at the door to listen, visualizing the house's floorplan. The laundry room led to a hallway, which in turn led to the kitchen, breakfast nook, and dining room, past the stairs to the lower level. Living room to the right, with French doors leading to the upper deck. Bedrooms to the left down another hallway. Access to the panic room was through the master and down a short hallway, located in the back of the walk-in closet.

She cracked the door and paused. Hearing nothing, she

slipped from the room into the hallway and made her way forward into the main house. The blood spatters had disappeared. Salome must have snagged a towel to stanch the bleeding on her way through the laundry room.

Leine scanned the living room. Nothing. She eased away from the living room and turned, taking in the kitchen sink, counter, oven, and hallway. No one was there.

She realigned the grip on her gun and slowed her breathing. Staying low, she moved toward the bedrooms. As she passed the entrance to the kitchen, she caught sight of two figures sitting at a table in the nook near the windows. She continued past and then stopped, her back to the wall.

Jinn and Nita.

Where was Salome?

Laser-focused, Leine eased around the doorway. There was a sharp intake of breath.

"Leine," Jinn whispered.

Leine crossed the floor to where Jinn and Nita were sitting and dropped to a crouch. She pushed up the NVGs as she slid her knife free to cut through the plastic ties binding them to the chairs.

"She's here somewhere," Nita warned, her voice low.

"I shot her, but I'm not sure if it's enough to slow her down."

"We heard something in the garage." Nita hesitated. "Was it Lou?"

Leine nodded. "He's alive."

"Thank God." Freed from the restraints, Nita rose from her chair.

Leine grasped her arm. "We need to get you and Jinn to the panic room. Now."

"I have to go to my husband."

"We don't know where she is."

"There's a loaded gun locked in the glove box in the truck. If I can get to the garage without her knowing..."

Leine nodded. Nita knew her way around guns. It was one of the things that had attracted Lou to her in the first place. At least the two of them would have some protection if Salome decided to pay a visit. "Fine. Be careful."

Nita nodded and disappeared into the dark hallway.

"I knew you would come," Jinn said. She leaned in close and whispered, "She wants to kill you."

Leine tossed the plastic ties on the floor. "I'll be all right. But first we need to get you to safety. Follow me. And stay low."

They moved quickly down the hall to the master bedroom. Leine cleared the room and master bath and led Jinn to the back of the walk-in closet. She swept aside a rack of clothing to reveal the door leading to the panic room and punched a code into the digital keypad. The lock clicked open, and she eased the door wide. Jinn slipped inside and turned to look at Leine.

"How do I get out?" she asked.

"Just turn the handle. There isn't a code. But wait until I give you the all clear. Don't open it for anyone except me, Lou, or Nita, okay?"

"Okay."

Leine closed the door and moved toward the outer hallway, her mind focused on finding Salome. As she crossed the threshold, there was a blur of motion. Leine dropped to a crouch and raised her weapon. Salome exploded from the hall, firing as she went.

Pain seared her right arm, and her hand went numb. Immediately shifting the gun to her left hand, she fired several rounds. At least one slammed into Salome's torso. Another hit her right forearm.

Both guns locked open at the same time. With a deep growl,

Salome lobbed her pistol at Leine and launched herself on top of her. The two women fell to the floor and rolled.

Ignoring the pain, Leine fought her with sharp jabs to the throat. Salome grabbed a handful of Leine's hair and gave it a vicious yank. She craned her neck forward, teeth exposed. Before Salome could take a bite of her carotid, Leine scissored her legs around the other woman's torso, hooked her ankles, and squeezed with everything she had.

Salome's eyes saucered, and she threw her head back, writhing in agony. Blood streamed from the gunshot wound in her abdomen. Sucking in a deep breath, she pitched forward and slammed her forehead into Leine's.

A flash of light and dark spots filled Leine's vision. Momentarily stunned, her grip on Salome loosened, and the terrorist rolled free. Shaking her head to clear it, Leine sprang to her feet, sliding her knife from its sheath as she did.

A blade flashed in her opponent's left hand.

"So this is how it ends," Salome said, smiling. Her ragged breathing echoed through the room. Blood saturated her clothes.

Leine's arm throbbed like a bitch, and she could tell her own blood loss had weakened her. "May the better woman win."

The two women circled each other like confined scorpions. Leine feinted to Salome's left. The terrorist didn't fall for it and moved in for a direct hit. Leine shifted her stance. She wasn't fast enough. The blade sliced through her shirt, lacerating her upper arm. Fighting adrenaline fatigue, Leine clenched her jaw and went after the other woman with a vengeance, slicing and cutting and feinting right, then left, then right again. Salome parried each attack but was unable to get in any of her own.

Her opponent appeared to get a second wind. In a surprise move, she countered Leine's attack and drove her backward, slashing wildly. Leine fended her off, avoiding the worst of the blade, but sustained dozens of cuts to her forearm and hand.

Continuing her relentless attack, Salome forced Leine backward into the closet. Leine stole a quick glance behind her, narrowly missing the built-in dresser as she parried the other woman's attack. Blood flowed freely from the wounds in Salome's torso and right hand, but her energy didn't flag. Narrowing her eyes, she stabbed the knife once, twice, a third time. With each thrust, Leine stepped back, circling the dresser, trying to position herself for a counterattack.

Recognizing her plan, Salome growled in rage. She doubled her efforts for a moment, then dropped to the floor and swept her leg in a wide arc, catching Leine by surprise.

Leine's feet went out from under her, and she landed on her back with a hard thud. A split-second later, Salome was on top of her, knee pinning her right arm to the floor, her knife arcing above Leine's face. Leine managed to grab the other blade as it plunged toward her, the hot burn of the razor-sharp edge slicing her palm. She held fast, certain the knife would sever her hand, but she didn't care. She wouldn't—couldn't let Salome win.

This was it—she had to defeat this woman or everyone she ever loved would die.

There was a loud click and the panic room door opened. Leine ignored it, as did Salome.

"Get off of her!"

The panic and rage in Jinn's voice pierced Leine's heart.

"Get back in the room," Leine yelled.

Jinn launched herself into the air and landed on Salome's back, clawing and kicking and screaming, her hands clutched around her throat.

Leine used the distraction to wrench the knife away, torqueing Salome's hand in a vicious twist. There was a loud *snap* and Salome screamed. She rose up and threw herself against the dresser, slamming Jinn into the hard surface. Jinn let go of Salome's throat and slid to the floor.

A spark of adrenaline surged through Leine. She rolled to her feet and lunged for her opponent. Salome turned to fend off the attack, but Leine was too quick and buried the blade in her stomach.

Salome sucked in a breath, her eyes wide with disbelief. She clutched at Leine's hand, trying to draw the blade from her body. Showing no mercy, Leine drove the weapon deeper and twisted, the other woman's warm, sticky blood cascading down her hand and the hilt of the knife.

As the life left her eyes, Salome slumped to the floor, mouth open as if to speak. Leine felt her neck for a pulse.

There was none. In another part of the house a door slammed open, followed by shouting and several footsteps.

Leine rushed to where Jinn sat crumpled at the base of the dresser, struggling to breathe. "Are you all right?"

Jinn nodded.

"Had the wind knocked out of you?"

Again, the girl nodded.

Relieved, Leine checked her ribs, back, and everywhere else she could for broken bones. Thankfully, the kid appeared intact.

Jinn gestured toward her bloody hand and shoulder. "Are you all right?" she wheezed, still trying to catch her breath.

"I'm fine. Thanks to you."

Seconds later, at least a half-dozen SWAT team members swarmed the bedroom.

"Show me your hands," the lead officer bellowed.

Leine raised her good arm. Eyes wide, Jinn followed suit and raised both hands.

"Are they all right?" Nita called from the other room. "Can I go in?"

"Not until we secure the area, ma'am," someone ordered.

"Oh, for heaven's sake," came her annoyed reply. "At least tell me if they're all right."

"We're fine, Nita," Leine called, and gave Jinn a tired smile.

"Who's this?" asked a man in full tactical gear, indicating Salome's lifeless, blood-soaked body.

"She called herself Salome," Leine replied. "As for her real name, your guess is as good as mine."

45

Six months later—SHEN Training Center, San Pedro, California

"Good job, Jinn," Leine called over the clamor of students practicing hand-to-hand combat in the open space of the warehouse. Jinn smiled and ducked her head in acknowledgement, her cheeks growing pink from the praise. Her instructor, Kathy McNabb, grinned. The SHEN operative had been happy to sign on to become a part-time trainer at the facility.

The kid was a natural, Leine thought. Scrappy, persistent, and smart. Jinn would be a huge asset to the SHEN team. And Leine would rest easier knowing she'd been well-trained.

Blue throwing mats covered the floor of the warehouse, allowing for a softer landing than the real world. Once students had graduated from the first six modules, they would be trained on wood, concrete, and tile. There would also be modules on shoot-or-don't-shoot, a driving course, how to use lock picks, and how to hotwire a car. Every student was required to learn at least one language other than English and would be dropped in the city of their choice to prove their proficiency.

Leine continued her circuit through the cluster of students, offering encouragement and stepping in when a participant or instructor needed help. Other operatives Leine had worked with when following Dmitry to the safe house had signed on as instructors: Miguel, Vernon, and Recker had all jumped at the chance to work with Leine on the new venture. Lou Stokes, having recovered from his knife wound, immediately warmed to the idea of training the next generation of SHEN operatives in hand-to-hand combat, firearms, and explosives.

It was a brutal world they worked in—the more training, the better.

At one end of the room her daughter, April, instructed a beginner in the program on the proper stance and actions when dealing with a larger adversary. Leine insisted that advanced students take on at least one beginner, more if they could handle it. Building trust between team members was paramount to the organization's mission.

Leine had learned that lesson the hard way.

She checked the time on her phone—the special guest she'd lined up for today's workshop would be there any minute. She glanced in the mirror that ran along the back wall and tucked an errant wisp of hair behind her ear.

The lacerations on her hands and arms from the knife fight with Salome had begun to fade, leaving a thin, white mosaic of scars. The gunshot wound on her upper arm had healed quickly, although there would always be evidence of the encounter with Salome—in the form of a small divot where the round had destroyed a chunk of skin and adipose tissue. Leine had been lucky the bullet didn't penetrate bone. Thank God she didn't have to wear the damned sling anymore.

Leine exited the larger room through double doors and walked to the facility's entrance. On the way she passed two larger rooms set aside for meditation and Yoga practice that were available to students any time there wasn't a class being taught. Leine loved stepping inside the soundproofed, sparsely furnished rooms, as they allowed her to remove herself from the intensity of the training facility.

And her life.

Several classrooms were scattered throughout the facility. Leine and Lou had both tapped their contact lists to find instructors with specialized knowledge to share with new recruits. When Leine pitched the center to Lou, she'd assured him she wanted a different kind of training facility—one that considered every aspect of being an operative for the anti-trafficking organization and took the whole person into consideration. She'd insisted that all recruits submit to mental, emotional, and physical evaluations at the beginning, middle, and end of the course. The curriculum was demanding, and she wanted to ensure everyone got a fair shake.

As she passed the reception desk, a door to one of the meditation rooms opened and Spencer Simms walked out. He eased the door closed behind him and fell into stride with her.

"The little shit's doing well, isn't she?" he asked, meaning Jinn.

"That she is."

"When do I get to inflict my little nuggets of wisdom on her?"

"Soon, Spencer. Soon."

After Simms sent her the photograph of one very dead Nigel Cripps along with the audio recording, Leine had asked him if he'd be interested in becoming a part-time instructor at the SHEN Training Center. She hadn't expected him to accept. He jumped at the chance.

"Ever since I left the agency," he'd explained, "I've been searching for something I assumed didn't exist. I thought money and being the captain of my own ship was enough. Turns out I needed a mission with purpose."

Now he trained advanced students in weapons and explosives. When he'd first devised his part of the course, April had insisted on being his guinea pig and made it through with flying colors. Apparently her daughter had the same natural tendencies as her mother.

Go figure.

"Good," Simms said, nodding. "I think the earlier we get the kid started, the better. She'll be a pro in no time."

Leine gave him a sharp look. "As long as you keep in mind she's eleven years old."

Simms waved her concerns away. "Don't worry. I'm not going to push her beyond her capabilities. At least, not right away." He smiled, teeth brilliantly white against his suntanned face. He'd taken to living the Southern California lifestyle and had learned to surf. Recently, he'd been making noises about staying on permanently.

She could live with that. He was a good addition to the team.

A white pickup turned off the main street and headed toward the warehouse. Leine stepped outside and waited for Lou and his passenger to climb from the vehicle.

The passenger turned toward Leine, and she caught her breath. Those green eyes always made her weak in the knees. It was just something she couldn't control. Not now, not ever.

Santiago Jensen smiled as he walked up the steps to greet Leine. He still had a slight limp, but it had improved a lot since the last time she'd seen him. Lou stayed back, pretending to fuss with something inside his truck.

"Hey," Santa said, his voice flowing over her like honey.

"Hey," she said back. They stood face-to-face for a few moments, looking into each other's eyes. Leine's heartbeat sped up and her cheeks warmed.

She cleared her throat and stepped back. "Thanks for coming. It means a lot."

Santa gave her the slow smile that always melted her. "Wouldn't miss it. Any time the LAPD can help an organization as worthy as SHEN, I'm all for it."

"I'm glad." Leine smiled. "They're just finishing up. You can set up at either end of the large room."

Santa nodded. He lifted his gaze and their eyes locked. Ignoring the impulse to fan herself, Leine shifted her stance and glanced at Lou. Part of her wanted him to interrupt them, part of her didn't.

A much bigger part, if she was being honest.

Santa followed her gaze and then returned his attention to Leine. "They found the Bomb Maker."

"Oh?"

He nodded. "The guy turned up at the safe house a couple of weeks ago. He was extradited to Riyadh. Apparently the Saudis wanted him back in a big way."

"When's the execution?"

"Knowing how fast they work over there, I'd say he's already sleeping with the scorpions."

"Couldn't have happened to a nicer guy."

"Yeah." Santa cleared his throat. He waited a beat before he said, "I know we both decided to give each other space."

"Right." Leine nodded. Their last conversation had taken place the week after the explosion at the warehouse. They'd both decided they needed time to heal from their wounds, including the ones Leine had inflicted on the relationship. Santa had graduated from therapy for the gunshot wound to his thigh a couple of months prior but still had a long way to go with this shoulder.

"I was wondering if maybe, after my talk"—Santa gestured toward the warehouse—"we could get a coffee or something."

Leine took a deep breath and let it go, suppressing her immediate impulse to suggest something other than coffee.

"I'd like that," she replied, her tone measured.

The smile he gave her acted as a balm to her soul, and was the only absolution Leine would ever need.

Ready for more? **Read Dakota Burn,** *the next heart-stopping Leine Basso thriller.*

ACKNOWLEDGMENTS

Thank you to everyone who helped me on the journey to The End: First reader and winner of the best supporting partner award, Mark Lindstrom—you ROCK; editing team extraordinaire Ruth Ross and Laurie Boris—this book wouldn't be as error-free without your help and super-human attention to detail; SFD aka TSODA 134—your expertise in all things military saves me every. single. time.; long-time writing partners Jenni, Ali, and Michelle—thanks for putting up with my crappy early drafts; Brian Yelland—ditto; Don Donnelly for electrical expertise; lovely and talented early readers Dawn and Barry Gill, for consistency and all things British; my fabulous Advance Reader Team—you guys are amazing and make these books so much better; and to everyone who buys indie—your support is crucial—thank you, thank you, thank you!

Writing is never a solitary endeavor.

ABOUT THE AUTHOR

DV Berkom is the USA Today bestselling author of two action-packed thriller series featuring strong female leads: Leine Basso and Kate Jones. Her love of creating resilient, kick-ass women characters stems from a lifelong addiction to reading spy novels, mysteries, and thrillers, and longing to find the female equivalent within those pages.

After years of moving around the country and skipping off to locations that could have been movie sets, she wrote her first novel and was hooked. Over a dozen novels later, she now makes her home in the Pacific Northwest with her husband, Mark, and several imaginary characters who like to tell her what to do.

Her most recent books include *Shadow of the Jaguar, Dakota Burn, Absolution, Dark Return, The Last Deception, Vigilante Dead*, and *A Killing Truth*. Currently, she's hard at work on her next thriller.

***Go to http://bit.ly/DVB_RL to join DV's exclusive Readers' List and be the first to know about new releases and subscriber-only offers.

ALSO BY D.V. BERKOM

Made in the USA
Middletown, DE
08 October 2020